Laicus

Lyman Abbott

Contents

LAICUS

BY
Lyman Abbott

PREFACE.

This book was not made; it has grown.

When three years ago I left the pulpit to engage in literary work and took my seat among the laity in the pews, I found that many ecclesiastical and religious subjects presented a different aspect from that which they had presented when I saw them from the pulpit. I commenced in the CHRISTIAN UNION in a series of "Letters from a Layman," to discuss from my new point of view some questions which are generally discussed from the clerical point of view alone. The letters were kindly received by the public. To some of the characters introduced I became personally attached. And the series of letters, commenced with the expectation that they might last through six or eight weeks, extended over a period of more than a year and a half--might perhaps have extended to the present it other duties had not usurped my time and thoughts.

This was the beginning.

But after a time thoughts and characters which presented themselves in isolated forms, and so were photographed for the columns of the newspaper, began to gather in groups. The single threads that had been spun for the weekly issue, wove themselves together in my imagination into the pattern of a simple story, true as to every substantial fact, yet fictitious in all its dress and form. And so out of Letters of Layman grew, I myself hardly know how, this simple story of a layman's life in a country parish.

I cannot dismiss this book from my table without adding that I am conscious that the deepest problem it discusses is but barely touched upon. This has obtruded itself upon the pattern in the weaving. It was intended for a single thread; but it has given color and character to all the rest. How shall Christian faith meet the current rationalism of the day? Not by argument; this is the thought I hope may be taught, or at least suggested, by the story of Mr. Gear's experience,--and it is a true not a fictitious story, except as all here is fictitious, i.e. in the external dress in which it is clothed. The very essence of rationalism is that it assumes that the reason is the highest faculty in man and the lord of all the rest. Grant this, as too often our controversial theology does grant it, and the battle is yielded before it is begun. Whether that rationalism leads to orthodox or heterodox conclusions, whether it issues in a Westminster Assembly's Confession of faith or a Positivist Primer is a matter of secondary importance. Religion is not a conclusion of the reason. The reason is not the lord of the spiritual domain. There is a world which it never sees and with which it is wholly incompetent to deal. And Christian faith wins its victories only when by its own--heart life it gives some glimpse of this hidden world and sends the rationalist, Columbus-like, on an unknown sea to search for this unknown continent.

I am not sure whether this preface had not better have remained unwritten; whether the parable had not better be left without an interpretation. But it is written and it shall stand. And so this simple story goes from my hands, I trust to do some little good, by hinting to clerical readers how some problems concerning Christian work appear to a layman's mind, and by quickening lay readers to share more generously in their pastors' labors and to understand more sympathetically their pastor's trials.

LYMAN ABBOTT.
The Knoll, Cornwall on the Hudson, N. Y.

LAICUS.

CHAPTER I.
How I happened to go to Wheathedge.

ABOUT sixty miles north of New York city,--not as the crow flies, for of the course of that bird I have no knowledge or information sufficient to form a belief, but as the Mary Powell ploughs her way up the tortuous channel of the Hudson river,--lies the little village of Wheathedge. A more beautiful site even this most beautiful of rivers does not possess. As I sit now in my library, I raise my eyes from my writing and look east to see the morning sun just rising in the gap and pouring a long golden flood of light upon the awaking village below and about me, and gilding the spires of the not far distant city of Newtown, and making even its smoke ethereal, as though throngs of angels hung over the city unrecognized by its too busy inhabitants. Before me the majestic river broadens out into a bay where now the ice-boats play back and forth, and day after day is repeated the merry dance of many skaters--about the only kind of dance I thoroughly believe in. If I stand on the porch upon which one of my library windows opens, and look to the east, I see the mountain clad with its primeval forest, crowding down to the water's edge. It looks as though one might naturally expect to come upon a camp of Indian wigwams there. Two years ago a wild-cat was shot in those same woods and stuffed by the hunters, and it still stands in the ante-room of the public school, the first, and last, and only contribution to an incipient museum of natural history which the sole scientific enthusiast of Wheathedge has founded--in imagination. Last year Harry stumbled on a whole nest of rattlesnakes, to his and their infinite alarm--and to ours too when afterwards he told us the story of his adventure. If I turn and look to the other side of the river, I see a broad and laughing valley,--grim in the beautiful death of winter now however,--through which the Newtown railroad, like the Star of Empire, westward takes its way. For the village of Wheathedge, scattered along the mountain side, looks down from its elevated situation on a wide expanse of country. Like Jerusalem of old,--only, if I can judge anything from the accounts of Palestinian travelers, a good deal more so,--it is beautiful for situation, and deserves to be the joy of the whole earth.

A village I have called it. It certainly is neither town nor city. There is a little centre where there is a livery stable, and a country store with the Post Office attached, and a blacksmith shop, and two churches, a Methodist and a Presbyterian, with the promise of a Baptist church in a lecture-room as yet unfinished. This is the old centre; there is another down under the hill where there is a dock, and a railroad station, and a great hotel with a big bar and generally a knot of loungers who evidently do not believe in the water-cure. And between the two there is a constant battle as to which shall be the town. For the rest, there is a road wandering in an aimless way along the hill-side, like a child at play who is going nowhere, and all along this road are scattered every variety of dwelling, big and little, sombre and gay, humble and pretentious, which the mind of man ever conceived of,--and some of which I devoutly trust the mind of man will never again conceive. There are solid substantial Dutch farm-houses, built of unhewn stone, that look as though they were outgrowths of the mountain, which nothing short of an earthquake could disturb; and there are fragile little boxes that look as though they would be swept away, to be seen no more forever, by the first winter's blast that comes tearing up the gap as though the bag of Eolus had just been opened at West Point and the imprisoned winds were off with a whoop for a lark. There are houses in sombre grays with trimmings of the same; and there are houses in every variety of color, including one that is of a light pea-green, with pink trimmings and blue blinds. There are old and venerable houses, that look as though they might have come over with Peter Stuyvesant and been living at Wheathedge ever since; and there are spruce little sprigs of houses that look as though they had just come up from New York to spend a holiday, and did not rightly know what to do with themselves in the country. There are staid and respectable mansions that never move from the even tenor of their ways; and there are houses that change their fashions every season, putting on a new coat of paint every spring; and there is one that dresses itself out in summer with so many flags and streamers that one might imagine Fourth of July lived there.

All nations and all eras appear also to be gathered here. There are Swiss cottages with overhanging chambers, and Italian villas with flat roofs, and Gothic structures with incipient spires that look as though they had stopped in their childhood and never got their growth, and Grecian temples with rows of wooden imitations of marble pillars of Doric architecture, and one house in which all nations and eras combine--a Grecian porch, a Gothic roof, an Italian L, and a half finished tower of the Elizabethan era, capped with a Moorish dome, the whole approached through the stiffest of all stiff avenues of evergreens, trimmed in the latest French fashion. That is Mr. Wheaton's residence, the millionaire of Wheathedge. I wish I could say he was as Catholic as his dwelling house.

I never fancied the country. Its numerous attractions were no attractions to me. I cannot harness a horse. I am afraid of a cow. I have no fondness for chickens--unless they are tender and well-cooked. Like the man in parable, I cannot dig. I abhor a hoe. I am fond of flowers but not of dirt, and had rather buy them than cultivate them. Of all ambition to get the earliest crop of green peas and half ripe strawberries I am innocent. I like to walk in my neighbor's garden better than to work in my own. I do not drink milk, and I do drink coffee; and I had rather run my risk with the average of city milk than with the average of country coffee. Fresh air is very desirable; but the air on the bleak hills of the Hudson in March is at times a trifle too fresh. The pure snow as it lies on field, and fence, and tree, is beautiful, I confess. But when one goes out to walk, it is convenient to have the sidewalks shoveled.

At least that is what I used to think five years ago. And if my wife had endeavored to argue me out of my convictions, she would only have strengthened them. But my wife:--

Stop a minute. I may as well say here that this book is written in confidence. It is personal. It deals with the interior history of a very respectable church and some most respectable families. It contains a great deal that is not proper to be communicated to the public. The reader will please bear this in mind. Whatever I say, particularly what I am going to say now, is confidential. Don't mention it.

My wife is a diplomate. If ever I am president of the United States--which may Heaven forbid,--she shall be secretary of State. She never argues; but she always carries her point.

She always lets me have my own way without hinting an objection. But it always ends in her having her own. She would have made no objection to letting Mason and Slidell go--not the least in the world. But she would have somehow induced England to entreat us to take them back--I am sure of it. She would not have dismissed Catacazy--not she. But if she did not like Catacazy, Gortschakoff should have recalled him, and never known why he did it.

"John," said my wife, "where shall we spend the summer?"

It was six years ago this spring. We were sitting in the library in our city house, Harry was a baby; and baby was not. I laid down the Evening Post, and looked up with an incipient groan.

"The usual way I suppose," said I. "You'll go home with the baby, and I--I shall camp out in New York."

"Home" is Jennie's home in Michigan, where she had spent two of the three summers of our married life, while I existed in single misery in my empty house in 38th street. Oh, the desolateness of those summer experiences. Oh, the unutterable loneliness of a house without the smile of the dear wife, and the laugh and prattle of the baby boy. I even missed his cry at night.

"It's a long, long journey," said Jennie, "and a long, long way off; and I did resolve last summer I never would put a thousand miles again between me and my true home, John. For that is not my home--you are my home."

And a soft hand stole gently up and toyed with my hair.

Vanity of vanities, all is vanity, saith the preacher. To which I add, especially husbands. No man is proof against the flatteries of love. At least I am not, and I am glad of it.

"You can't stay here, Jennie," said I.

"I am afraid not," said she. "It is Harry's second summer, and I would not dare."

"The sea shore?" said I, interrogatively.

"Not one of those great fashionable hotels, John. It would be worse for Harry than the city. And then think of the cost."

"True," said I reflectively. "I wish we could find a quiet place, not too far from the city so that I could come in and out during term time, and stay out altogether during the summer vacation."

"There must be some such, many such," said Jennie.

"But to look for them," said I, "would be, to use an entirely new simile, like looking for a needle in a haystack. There must be some honest lawyers at the New York bar, and some impartial judges on the New York bench, but I should not like to be set to find them."

I had been beaten in an important case that afternoon and was out with my profession.

"Suppose you let me try," said Jennie--"that is to find the quiet summer retreat, not the honest lawyer."

"By all means, my dear," said I. "And I have great confidence that if you are patient and assiduous, you will find a place in time for Harry to settle down in comfortably when he gets ready to be married."

Jennie laughed a quiet little laugh at my incredulity, and sat straightway down to write half a dozen letters of inquiry to as many different friends in the environs of New York. I resumed the Evening Post. As to anything coming of her plans I no more dreamt of it than your grandfather, reader, dreamt of the Atlantic cable.

But though I had been married three years I did not know Jennie then as well as I know her now. I have since learned that she has a habit of accomplishing what she undertakes. But this again is strictly confidential.

That June saw us snugly ensconced at Mr. Lines'. Glen-Ridge is the euphonious title he has given to his pretty but unpretending place. Jennie had written among others to Sophie Wheaton, n,e Sophie Nichols, an old school-fellow, and Sophie had sent down an invitation to her to come and spend a week and look for herself, and she had done so; save that two days had sufficed instead of a week. Glen-Ridge had taken her fancy, Mr. Lines had met her housewifely idea of a good house-keeper, and she had selected the rooms and agreed on terms, and left nothing for me to do except to ratify the bargain by a letter, which I did the day after her return. And so in the early summer of 1866 the diplomate had carried her first point, and committed me to two months' probation in the country; and two very delightful months they were.

CHAPTER II.
More Diplomacy.

I now verily believe that Jennie from the first had made up her mind that we were to settle in Wheathedge. Though I never liked the country, she did. And I now think that summer at Wheathedge was her first step toward a settlement there. But she never hinted it to me.

Not she. On the contrary, she often went down to the city with me, and short-ened the car ride by half. We kept the city house open. She exercised a watchful supervision over the cook. The sheets were not damp, the coffee was not muddy, the library table was not covered with dust. I blessed her a hundred times a week for the love that found us both this Wheathedge home, and made the city home so comfortable and cosy. Yet I came to my house in the city less and less. The car ride grew shorter every week. When the courts closed and the long vacation, ar-rived I bade the cook an indefinite good-bye. My clients had to conform to the new office hours, 10 to 3, with Saturdays struck off the office calendar, and, in the dog days, Mondays too. Yet I was within call, and business ran smoothly. The country looked brighter than it used to do. I learned to enjoy the glorious sunrise that New Yorkers never see. I discovered that there were other indications of a moonlight night than the fact that the street lamps were not lighted. Harry grew fat and rosy, and his little chuckle developed into a lusty laugh. Jennie's headaches were blown away by the fresh air that came down from the north. I found the fragrance of the new mown hay from the Glen-Rridge meadow more agreeable than the fragrant odors which the westerly winds waft over to Murray Hill from the bone boiling establishments of the Hudson river. Every evening Jennie met me at the train with Tom--Mr. Lines' best horse, whom I liked so well that I hired him for the season; and we took long drives and renewed the scenes of five years before, when Jennie was Jennie Malcolm, and I was just graduating from Harvard law-school. And still the diplomate never hinted at the idea of making a home at Wheathedge.

But one day as we drove by Mr. Sinclair's she remarked casually, "What a pret-ty place!"

It was a pretty place. A little cottage, French gray with darker trimmings of the same; the tastiest little porch with a something or other--I know the vine by sight but not to this day by name--creeping over it, and converting it into a bower; another porch fragrant with climbing roses and musical with the twittering of young swallows who had made their nests in little chambers curiously constructed under the eaves and hidden among the sheltering leaves; a green sward sweeping down to the road, with a few grand old forest trees scattered carelessly about as though nature had been the landscape gardner; and prettiest of all, a little boy and girl playing horse upon the gravel walk, and filling the air with shouts of merry laughter--all this combined to make as pretty a picture as one would wish to see. The western sun poured a flood of light upon it through crimson clouds, and a soft glory from the dying day made this little Eden of earth more radiant by a baptism from heaven.

I wonder now if Jennie had been waiting for a favorable opportunity and then had spoken. I do not know; and she will never tell me. At all events the beauty so struck me, like a landscape fresh from the hand of some great artist--as it was indeed, fresh from the hand of the Great Artist--that I involuntarily reined in Tom to look at it. "It's for sale, too," said I, "I wonder what such a place costs."

The artful diplomate did not answer. The books and newspapers talk about women's curiosity. It's nothing to a man's curiosity when it is aroused. Oh, I know the story of Bluebeard very well. But if Mrs. Bluebeard had been a strong minded woman, and had killed her seven husbands, I wonder if the eighth would not have taken a peep. He would not have waited for the key but would have broken in the door long before. If men are not curious why do the authorities always appoint them on the detective police force?

"Mr. Lines," said I that evening at the tea table, "you know that pretty little cottage on the hill just opposite the church. I see there is a sign up 'for sale.' What is the price of it, do you know?"

"No," said Mr. Lines. "But you can easily find out. It belongs to Charlie Sinclair; he lives there and can tell you."

Three days after that, as I was driving up from the station, it struck my fancy I should like to see the inside of that pretty house. "Jennie," said I, "let's go in and look at the inside of that pretty cottage." But I had no more idea of purchasing it than I have now of purchasing the moon.

"It would hardly be the thing for me to call," said the diplomate. "Mrs. Sinclair has never called on me."

"I don't want you to make any call," said I. "The house is for sale. I am a New Yorker. I am looking about Wheathedge for a place. I see this place is for sale. I should like to look at it. And of course my wife must look at it too."

"Oh! that indeed," said my wife, "that's another matter. I have no particular objection to that."

"Besides," said I, "I really should like to know the price of such a place in Wheathedge."

"Very good," said Jennie.

So we drove up to the gate, fastened the horse, and inquired of Mrs. Sinclair, who came in person to the door, if we could see the house. Certainly. She would be very happy to show it to us. And a very pretty house it was--and is still. There was a cozy little parlor with a bay window looking out on the river, there was an equally cozy little dining-room, and there was an L for a sitting-room--which I instantly converted in my imagination into a library--which looked with one window on the river and with another on the mountains. There was a very convenient kitchen built out in a wing from one end of the dining-room, and three chambers over the three downstairs rooms, from the larger one of which, over the sitting-room, we could take in at a glance the Presbyterian church, the blacksmith's shop, and the country store, with the wandering and aimless road, and a score or two of neighbor's homes which lay along it; for the cottage was on the hillside, and elevated considerably above the main roadway. It was charmingly furnished too, and was full of the fragrance of flowers within, as it was embowered in them without.

Besides looking at the house we asked the usual house-hunting questions. Mr. Sinclair was in the city. He wanted to sell because he was going to Europe in the spring to educate his children. He would sell his place for $10,000 or rent it for $800. For the summer? No! for the year. He did not care to rent it for the summer, nor to give possession before fall. Would he rent the furniture? Yes, if one wanted it. But that would be extra. How much land was there? About two acres. Any fruit? Pears, peaches, and the smaller fruits--strawberries, raspberries, and blackberries. Whereupon Jennie and I bowed ourselves out and went away.

And nothing more was said about it till the next February. The diplomate still kept her own counsel.

Then I opened the subject. It was the evening of the first day of February. I had been in to pay my rent. "Jennie," said I, "the landlord raises our rent to $2,500.

"What are you going to do?" said she quietly; "pay it?"

"Pay it!" said I. "No. It's high at $2,000.--We shall have to move."

"Where to?" said Jennie.

I shrugged my shoulders. I had not the least idea.

"What are you going to do next summer?" said she.

"Glen-Ridge?" said I interrogatively.

"I am afraid I shall have to be in my own home next summer," said Jennie. "The mother cannot leave her nest to find a home among strangers when God sends her a little bird to be watched and tended. And I hope, John, God is going to send another little bird to our nest this summer."

"You shall have your own home, Jennie dear," said I. "I will tell the landlord to-morrow that we will keep it. But it is an imposition."

"I am so sorry to give up our summer at Wheathedge," said she. "We did enjoy ourselves so much, John, and Harry grew and thrived so."

"It can't be helped, Jennie," said I.

"No"--said she slowly, and as if thinking to herself; "no--unless we took the Sinclair cottage for the summer."

"I hadn't thought of that," said I.

"What was the rent?" asked the diplomate. She knew as well as I did.

"Eight hundred dollars a year," said I.

"That is a clear saving of $1,700 a year," said Jennie.

"That's a fact," said I.

"If we did not like it we could come back to the city in the fall, and get a house here; if we did we could stay later and come in to board for three or four months. I shouldn't mind if we did not come at all."

"No country in the winter for me, thank you," said I; "with the wind drawing through the open cracks in your country built house half freezing you, and when you try to keep warm your air-tight stove half suffocating you; with the roads outside blocked up with great drifts, and the trains delayed just on the days when I have a critical case in court."

"Very well," said Jennie. She is too much of a diplomate to argue. "When the snow comes we can easily move back again, as easily as find a new house now. To tell the truth, John, I have no heart for house-hunting now."

"Well," said I. "I will see Sinclair to-morrow. And if his house is in the market, Jennie, we we will move there as soon as the spring fairly opens."

It was in the market. He was anxious to be rid of it. I hired it for the year, together with the furniture, at $800,--and he agreed that if I bought it in the Fall the half year rent should go on the purchase money. I did not pay him any rent. I did not move into the city when the snow came. The diplomate had her own way as she always does. We live in the country; and I--I am very glad of it. I can harness Katie on a pinch. I am not afraid of the cow. I am not skilful with the hoe, but I am as proud of my flower garden as any of my neighbors. And as to the relative advantages of city and country, I am quite of the opinion of Harry.

"Harry," said his grandfather the other day, "don't you want to go back to the city and live?"

"No!" said Harry, with the utmost expression of scorn on his face.

"Why not, Harry?"

"It smells so."

CHAPTER III.
We join the Church.

"I have bought the house, Jennie," said I.

"Thank you," said Jennie. She said it softly, but her eyes said it more plainly than her voice. I had hesitated a little before I finally closed the purchase. But Jennie's look and her soft "Thank you" made me sure I had been right.

Since the baby has come we have converted the chamber over the library into an upstairs sitting-room. I found her there before the open fire, on my return from New York. The baby was sleeping in her arms; and she was gently rocking him, pressed close to her bosom.

"I wish you would have a nurse for the baby, Jennie," said I. "I don't like to see you tied to her so."

"You wouldn't take baby from me would you, John?" said she appealingly, nestling the precious bundle closer to her heart than before, as if in apprehension. No I wouldn't. I was obliged to confess that, to myself if not to her.

"John," said Jennie, "Mrs Goodsole has been here this afternoon. She wants to know if we won't take our letters to this church the next communion. It is the first of September."

"Well?" said I, for Jennie had stopped.

"She says that if we are going to make Wheathedge our home she hopes we can find a pleasant home in the church here. I told her I could not tell, we had only hired the house for the summer and might leave in the fall. But if you have bought it, John, and I am, oh! so glad you have and thank you so much"--one hand left the baby gently, and was laid on my arm with the softest possible pressure by way of emphasizing the thanks again,--"perhaps we ought to consider it."

"I have no notion of joining this church," said I. "It's in debt, and always behind hand. I am told they owe a hundred dollars to their minister now."

"That's too bad," said Jennie.

"And we can't do much if we do join it. I have no time for church affairs, and you--you have all you can do to attend to your infant class at home, Jennie."

"That's true," said Jennie.

"Besides it is a Presbyterian church and we are Congregationalists."

Jennie made no reply.

"And I can't bear the idea of leaving the Broadway Tabernacle church. I was brought up in it. I have been in its Sunday-School ever since I can recollect. It was dear to me in its old homely attire as a Congregationalist meeting-house. It is dear to me in its new aristocratic attire as a Congregationalist cathedral. And Harry was baptized there. And there are all our dearest and best friends. It would be like pulling a tooth to uproot from it."

"It is dear to me too, John," said Jennie softly, "for your sake, if not for my own."

"And all our friends are there, Jennie," continued I. "Except the Lines and Deacon Goodsole we hardly know anybody here."

"Though I suppose time will cure that," said Jennie.

"I do not know that I care to cure it," said I.

Jennie made no response.

Was it not at Bunker Hill that the soldiers were directed to reserve their fire till the attacking party had exhausted theirs? That is the way Jennie conducts an argument--when she argues at all, which is very seldom. She accepted every consideration I had offered against uniting with the Wheathedge church, and yet I knew her opinion was not changed; and somehow my own began to waver. I wonder how that method of arguing would work in the court-room. I mean to try it some time.

I had exhausted my fire and Jennie was still silent. Silence they say means consent. But I knew that it did not in her case. It depends so much upon the kind of silence.

"What do you say Jennie?" said I.

"Well, John," said she slowly and thoughtfully, "perhaps there are two sides to the question. I don't like to leave the Broadway Tabernacle. But it seems to me that we have left it. We cannot attend its prayer-meetings, or go to its Sabbath-school, or worship with its members on the Sabbath, or even mingle much with its members in social life. We have left it, and we ought to have thought of that before we left--not after. Perhaps I am to blame, John, that I did not think of it more. I did not think of what you were giving up for me when you took this beautiful home for my sake."

I had not taken it for her sake--that is, not wholly for her sake. And as to the giving up! Why, bless you, that little sitting-room, with the wife and baby it contained, was worth a thousand Tabernacles to me; and I managed to tell Jennie so, and emphasize the declaration with a--well no matter. But she did not need the information, she knew it very well before, I am sure.

"The real question seems to me, John, to be whether we mean to be church members at all?" said Jennie.

"Church members at all!" I echoed.

"Yes," said she. "We are not members of the Broadway Tabernacle any more--except in name. What is a foot or an arm fifty miles away from the body? Can they keep loving watch and care over us; or we over them? It is not a question between one church-home and another, John; it is a question between this church-home and none at all."

"But, Jennie," said I, "the finances here are in a fearful state. They are always coming down on the church for contributions, and holding fairs in summer, and tableaux and what not, in winter, and generally waiting for something to turn up. If I had the naming of this church I would call it St. Micawber's church."

Jennie laughed. "Well, John," said she, "I think you are ready enough with your money." (I am not so sure of that. I am inclined to think that is Jennie's way of making me so.) "And I have nothing to say about the finances."

"Besides, Jennie," said I--for I really had no faith in the financial argument--"this is a Presbyterian church and we are Congregationalists."

"It is a church of Christ, John," said Jennie soberly, "and we, I hope, are Christians more than Congregationalists."

That was the last that was said. But the next morning I carried down with me, to New York, a letter addressed to the clerk of the Broadway Tabernacle, asking for letters of dismission and recommendation to the Calvary Presbyterian church at Wheathedge. And so commenced our parish life.

CHAPTER IV.
The Real Presence.

"JENNIE," said I, "I don't believe in Mr. Work's sermon this morning, do you?"

"I don't think I do, John; but to be candid I did not hear a great deal of it."

It was Sunday evening. Harry was asleep in his room. The baby, sung to her sweet slumbers pressed against her mother's heart, had been lain down at last in her little cradle. Jennie, her evening work finished, had come down into the library and was sitting on the lounge beside me.

"I was not so fortunate," said I. "Blessed are those who having ears hear not--sometimes. I listened, and took the other side. My church was converted into a court-room, I into an advocate. If I believed Mr. Work's doctrine was sound Protestantism I should turn Roman Catholic. Its teaching is the warmer, cheerier, more helpful of the two."

Then I took up the open book that lay on my library table and read from Father Hyacinthe's discourses the following paragraph--from an address delivered on the first communion of a converted Protestant to the Roman Catholic Church:

"Where (in Protestantism) is that real Presence which flows from the sacrament as from a hidden spring, like a river of peace, upon the true Catholic, all the day long, gladdening and fertilizing all his life? This Immanuel--God with us--awaited you in our Church, and in that sacrament which so powerfully attracted you, even when you but half believed it. In your own worship, as in the ancient synagogue, you found naught but types and shadows; they spoke to you of reality, but did not contain it; they awakened your thirst, but did not quench it; weak and empty rudiments which have no longer the right to rest, since the veil of the temple has been rent asunder and eternal realities been revealed."

"Yes, Jennie," said I. "If I thought Father Hyacinthe were right, I should turn Roman Catholic. And Mr. Work this morning confirmed him. He took away the substance. He left us only a type, a shadow."

The sermon was on the words--"Do this in remembrance of me." It was a doctrinal sermon. I am not sure that it might not have been a useful one--in the sixteenth century. It was a sermon against Romanism and Lutheranism and High Church episcopacy. The minister told us what were the various doctrines of the communion. He analyzed them and dismissed them one after another. He showed very conclusively, to us Protestants, that the Romanists are wrong, to us Presbyterians that the Episcopalians are wrong, to us who are open Communionists that the close Communionists are wrong. As there does not happen to be either Romanist, Episcopalian, or close Communionist in our congregation, I cannot say how efficacious his arguments would have been if addressed to any one who was in previous doubt as to his conclusions. Then he proceeded to expound what he termed the rational and Scriptural doctrine of communion. It is, he told us, simply a memorial service. It simply commemorates the past. "As," said he, "every year, the nation gathers to strew flowers upon the graves of its patriot soldiers, so this day the Christian Church gathers to strew with flowers of love and praise the grave of the Captain of our salvation. As in the one act all differences are forgotten, and the nation is one in the sacred presence of death, so in the other, creeds and doctrines vanish, and the Church of Christ appears at the foot of Calvary as one in Christ Jesus."

Mr. Wheaton asked me, as we came out of church, if the sermon was not a magnificent one. I evaded the question. I was obliged to confess to myself that it was unsatisfactory. If I were obliged to choose between the Protestantism of Mr. Work and the Romanism of Father Hyacinthe, I am afraid I should choose the latter.

"But," said Jennie, "Mr. Work's sermon was not true Protestant doctrine, John. There is a Real Presence in the communion. Only it is in the heart, not in the head, in us, not in the symbols that we eat. Did you not feel the Real Presence when Father Hyatt in the afternoon broke and blessed the bread? Did you not see the living Christ in his radiant face and hear the living Christ in his touching words, and his more touching silence?"

Yes! I did. Father Hyatt had disproved the morning's sermon, though he said never a word about it.

Father Hyatt is an old, old man. He has long since retired from active service, having worn out his best days here at Wheathedge, in years now long gone by. A little money left him by a parishioner, and a few annual gifts from old friends among his former people, are his means of support. His hair is white as snow. His hands are thin, his body bent, his voice weak, his eyesight dim, his ears but half fulfil their office; his mind even shows signs of the weakness and wanderings of old age; but his heart is young, and I verily believe he looks forward to the hour of his release with hopes as high and expectations as ardent as those with which, in college, he anticipated the hour of his graduation. This was the man, patriarch of the Church, who has lived to see the children he baptized grow up, go forth into the world, many die and be buried; who has baptized the second and even the third generation, and has seen Wheathedge grow from a cross-road to a flourishing village; who this afternoon, perhaps for the last time--I could not help thinking so as I sat in church--interpreted to us the love of Christ as it is uttered to our hearts in this most sacred and hallowed of all services. Very simply, very gently, quite unconsciously, he refuted the cheerless doctrine of the morning sermon, and pointed us to the Protestant doctrine of the Real Presence. Do you ask me what he said? Nothing. It was by his silence that he spoke.

A few tender, loving, reverential words as he broke the bread. Three minutes of silver speech, the rest of his part of the service a golden silence. But those few words were radiant with the presence and the love of a risen, a living Saviour. It was not of the Christ that died, but of the Christ that now lives, and intercedes, and guides, and preserves, and saves, he spoke, with voice feeble with old age, but strong with love. And as he spoke, it seemed to me, I think it seemed to all of us, that the Christ he loved so much and served so faithfully was close at hand, near and ready to bless us all, not with a sacred memory only, but with a Real Presence, the more real because unseen.

"Yes, Jennie," said I after we had sat for a few minutes in silence recalling that sacred hour, "Yes, Jennie, there was a Real Presence in Father Hyatt's breaking and blessing of the bread. But what do you say of the disquisition of Mr. Work on transubstantiation which followed it?"

"I didn't hear it, John. Was it really about transubstantiation? Perhaps I ought to have listened--but I could not, I did not want to. A higher, holier voice was speaking to me. I was absorbed in that. I was thinking how of old time Christ appeared in the breaking of bread to the disciples whose eyes were holden. And to-night, John, as I have been rocking baby to sleep I have been reading Tennyson's Holy Grail, and thinking how often, in our modern life, Calabad and Percivale kneel at the same shrine, and how often what is but a memorial service to the one affords a beatific vision of a living and life-giving Lord to the other."

And Jennie repeated in a low soft voice a verse from that strange poem, whose meaning, I sometimes think, is but half understood even by its admirers:

"And at the sacring of the Mass, I saw
The holy elements alone: but he
'Saw ye no more? I, Galahad, saw the Grail,
The Holy Grail, descend upon the shrine:
I saw the fiery face as of a child
That smote itself into the bread, and went,
And hither am I come; and never yet
Hath what thy sister taught me first to see
This holy thing, failed from my side?'"

"Ah! yes, John, Father Hyacinthe is mistaken, and Mr. Work is mistaken too. There is more in our communion than can be explained. The reason is a great deal, a great deal, but it is not everything. And there are experiences which it can neither understand nor interpret. Baby is not only up-stairs, John; he is in my heart of hearts. And you are never away from home, husband mine, though often in the city, but are always with me. And my Saviour he is not far away, he is not in the heaven that we must bring him down, nor in the past that we must summon him from centuries long gone by. He is in our hearts, John. Do I believe in the Real Presence? Do I not know that there is a Real Presence? And neither priest nor pastor can take it from me."

"I wish you could have administered the communion this afternoon, Jennie," said I, "instead of Mr. Work."

"I wish some good friend of Mr. Work would advise him not to talk at the communion," said Jennie.

"Write him a note," said I.

Jennie shook her head. "No," said she. "It would only do harm. But I wish ministers knew and felt that at the communion table there is a Real Presence that makes many words unfitting. When we are on the mount of Transfiguration, we do not care much for Peter, James or John. And so, dear, I recommend you to do as I do--if the minister must give us a doctrinal disquisition, or a learned argument, or an elaborate arabesque of fancy work, or an impassioned appeal, let him go his way and do not heed him. I want silence that I may commune with the Real Presence. If the minister does not give it me, I take it."

Jennie is right, I am sure. What we laymen want at the communion service, from our pastors, is chiefly silence. Only a few and simple words; the fewer and simpler the better. Oh! you who are privileged to distribute to us the emblems of Christ's love, believe me that the communion never reaches its highest end, save when you interpret it to us, not merely as a flower-strewn grave of a dead past, but as a Mount of Transfiguration whereon we talk with a living, an ascended Saviour. Believe me too, we want at that table no other message than that which a voice from on high whispers in our hearts: "This is my beloved Son, hear ye him!"

CHAPTER V.
Our Church Finances.

I FOUND one evening last week, in coming home, a business-like- looking letter lying on my library table. I rarely receive letters at Wheathedge; nearly all my correspondence comes to my New York office. I tore it open in some surprise and read the note as follows:

WHEATHEDGE, Oct. 9th.

"Dear Sir,--A meeting of the male members of the congregation of the Calvary Presbyterian Church will be held on Thursday evening, at 8 P. M., at the house of Mr. Wheaton. You are respectfully invited to be present.

"Yours, Respectfully,

"JAMES WHEATON, "Ch'n. B'd. Trustees."

"Well," said I to myself, "I wonder what this means. It can't be a male sewing society, I suppose. It can hardly be a prayer-meeting at Jim Wheaton's house. Male members! eh? I thought the female members carried on this church." In my perplexity, I handed the note to my wife. She read it with care. "Well," said she, "I am glad the people are waking up at last." "What does it mean?" said I. "It means money," said she. "Or rather it means the want of money. Mrs. Work told me last week she believed her husband would have to resign. All last quarter's salary is overdue, and something beside. It seems that Mr. Wheaton has begun to act, at last. I don't see what they want to make such men church officers for."

My wife has not very clear ideas about the legal relations which exist between the Church and the Society. Mr. Wheaton is an officer, not of the church but of the society; but I did not think it worth while to correct the mistake.

"I do want to think kindly of every body," said Jennie; "but it makes me indignant to see a minister defrauded of his dues."

"Defrauded is a pretty strong word, Jennie," said I.

"It is a true word," said she. "The people promise the minister $1200 a year, and then pay him grudgingly $900, and don't finally make up the other $300 till he threatens to resign; if that is not defrauding, I don't know what is. If Mr. Wheaton can't make the Board of Trustees keep their promises any better than that, he had better resign. I wish he would."

Mr. Wheaton is not a member of the church; and, to tell the truth, his reputation for success is greater than his reputation for integrity. But he is president of the Koniwasset branch railroad, and a leading director of the Koniwasset coal mines, and a large operator in stocks, and lives in one of the finest houses in Wheathedge, and keeps the handsomest carriage, and hires the most expensive pew, and it was considered quite a card, I believe, to get him to take the presidency of the Board of Trustees.

"Of course you'll go, John," said Jennie.

"I don't know about that, Jennie," said I. "I don't want to get mixed up with our church finances in their present condition."

"I don't know how they are ever to get in a better condition, John," said she, "unless some men like you do get mixed up with them."

Jennie, as usual, knew me better than I knew myself. I went. I was delayed just as I was starting away, and so, contrary to my custom--for I rather pride myself on being a very punctual man--I was a little late. The male members of the Calvary Presbyterian Congregation were already assembled in Mr. James Wheaton's library when I arrived. I was a little surprised to see how few male members we had. To look round the congregation on Sunday morning, one would certainly suppose there were more. It even seems to me there were at least twice as many at the sewing society when it met at James Wheaton's last winter.

I entered just as Mr. Wheaton was explaining the object of the meeting. "Gentlemen," said he, suavely, "the Calvary Presbyterian Church, like most of its neighbors, has rather hard work to get along, financially. Its income is not at all equal to its expenditures. The consequence is we generally stand on the debtor side of the ledger. As probably you know, there is a mortgage on the church of four thousand dollars. The semi-annual interest is due on the first of next month. There is, I think, no money in the treasury to meet it."

Here he looked at the treasurer as if for confirmation, and that gentleman, a bald-headed, weak-face man, smiled a mournful smile, and shook his head feebly.

"The Board of Trustees," continued the President, "have directed me to call this meeting and lay the matter before you."

There was a slight pause--a sort of expectant silence. "It isn't a large sum," gently insinuated the President, "if divided among us all. But, in some way, gentlemen, it must be raised. It won't do for us to be insolvent, you know. A church can't take the benefit of the bankrupt act, I believe, Mr. Laicus."

Being thus appealed to, I responded with a question. Was this mortgage interest all that the church owed? No! the President thought not. He believed there was a small floating debt beside. "And to whom," said I, "Mr. Treasurer, is this floating debt due?" The Treasurer looked to the President for an answer, and the President accepted his pantomimic hint.

"Most of it," said he, "I believe, to the minister. But I understand that he is in no special hurry for his money. In fact," continued he, blandly, "a debt that is due to the minister need never be a very serious burden to a church. Nominally it is due to him, but really it is distributed around among the members of the church. Part is due to the grocer, part to the tailor, part to the butcher, part to the dressmaker, and part is borrowed from personal friends. I lent the parson twenty-five dollars myself last week. But mortgage interest is another matter. That, you know, must be provided for."

"And pray," said I, for I happened to know the parson did need the money, "how much is the pastor's salary? And how much of it is overdue?"

"Well," said the President, "I suppose his salary is about--two thousand dollars. Yes," continued he, thoughtfully, somewhat affectionately playing with his gold watch-chain, "it must net him fully that amount."

I was wondering what this "about" meant, and whether the minister did not have a fixed salary, when Deacon Goodsole broke in abruptly with, "It's twelve hundred dollars a year!"

"Yes," responded the President, "it is nominally fixed by the Board at twelve hundred dollars. But then, gentlemen, the perquisites are something. In the course of a year they net up to a pretty large amount. Last winter, the ladies clubbed together and made the parson a present of carpets for his parlors; the year before we gave him a donation party; almost every year, Deacon Goodsole sends him a barrel of flour from his store; in one way or another he gets a good many similar little presents. I always send him a free pass over the road. And then there are the wedding fees which must amount to a handsome item in the course of the year. It can't be less than two thousand or twenty-five hundred dollars all told. A very snug little income, gentlemen."

"Double what I get," murmured Mr. Hardcap. A very exemplary gentleman is Mr. Hardcap, the carpenter, but more known for the virtue of economy than for any other. He lives in three rooms over his carpenter shop down in Willow lane. If our pastor lived there he would be dismissed very soon.

I wondered, as the President was speaking, whether he included the profit he made in selling Koniwasset coal to the Newtown railroad among his perquisitis, and as part of his salary. But I did not ask.

"Week before last," said Deacon Goodsole, "the parson was called to attend a wedding at Compton Mills. He drove down Monday, through that furious storm, was gone nearly all day, paid six dollars for his horse and buggy, and received five dollars wedding fee. I wonder how long it would take at that rate to bring his salary up to twenty-five hundred dollars."

There was a general laugh at the parson's mercantile venture, but no other response.

"Well, gentlemen," said the President, a little gruffly, I fancied, "let us get back to business. How shall we raise this mortgage interest? I will be one of ten to pay it off."

"Excuse me," said I, gently, "but before we begin to pay our debts, we must find out how much they are. Can the Treasurer tell us how much we owe Mr. Work?"

The Treasurer looked inquiringly at the President, but getting no response, found his voice, and replied, "Three hundred dollars."

"The whole of last quarter?" said I.

The Treasurer nodded.

"I think there is a little due on last year," said Deacon Goodsole.

"A hundred and seventy-five dollars," said the Treasurer.

"The fact is, gentlemen," said the President, resuming his blandest manner, "you know the Methodists have just got into their new stone church. The trustees thought it necessary not to be behind their neighbors, and so we have completely upholstered our church anew, at a cost of five hundred dollars." ("And made the parson pay the bill," said Deacon Goodsole, soto voce.) "We should have frescoed it, too, if we had had the money." ("Why didn't you take his wedding fees?" said the

Deacon, soto voce.)

"Well, for my part," said I, "I am willing to do my share toward paying off this debt. But I will not pay a cent unless the whole is paid. The minister must be provided for."

"I say so, too," murmured Mr. Hardcap. I was surprised at this sudden and unexpected reinforcement. The Deacon told me afterwards, that Mr. Hardcap had been repairing the parson's roof and had not got his pay.

"Perhaps," continued I, "we can fund this floating debt, make the mortgage four thousand five hundred, raise the difference among ourselves, and so clear it all up. Who holds the mortgage?"

This question produced a sensation like that of opening the seventh seal in heaven. There was silence for the space of--well, something less than half an hour. The Treasurer looked at the President. The President looked at the Treasurer. The male members of the congregation looked at each other. The Deacon looked at me with a very significant laugh lurking in the corners of his mouth. At length the President spoke.

"Well, gentlemen," said he, "I suppose most of you know I hold this mortgage. I have not called you together because I want to press the church for the money. But a debt, gentlemen, is a debt, and the church, above all institutions, ought to remember the divine injunction of our blessed Master (the President is not very familiar with Scripture, and may be excused the blunder): 'Owe no man anything.' ("Except the minister," said Deacon Goodsole, soto voce.) The proposition of our friend here, however, looks like business to me. I think the matter can be arranged in that way."

Arranged it was. The President got his additional security, and the parson got his salary, which was the main thing Jennie cared for. And to be perfectly frank with the reader, I should not have gone near Jim Wheaton's that night if it had not been that I knew it would please Jennie. I wait with some curiosity to see what will become of a church whose expenditures are regularly a quarter more than its income. Meanwhile, I wonder whether the personal presents which friends make for affection's sake to their pastor ought to be included by the Board of Trustees in their estimate of his salary? and also whether it is quite the thing to expect that the pastor will advance, out of his own pocket, whatever money is necessary to keep his church from falling behind its neighbors in showy attractions?

CHAPTER VI.
Am I a Drone?

DEACON Goodsole wants me to take a class in the Sabbath-school. So does Mr. Work. So I think does Jennie, though she does not say much. She only says that if I did she thinks I could do a great deal of good. I wonder if I could. I have stoutly resisted them so far. But I confess last Sunday's sermon has shaken me a little.

I was kept in the city Saturday night by a legal appointment, and went the next day to hear my old friend Thomas Lane preach. His text was "Why stand ye here all the day idle?"

He depicted very graphically the condition of the poor in New York. He is a man of warm sympathies, of a large and generous heart. He mingles a great deal with the poor of his own congregation. To his credit and that of his wife be it said, there are a good many poor in his congregation. But he does not confine his sympathies to his own people. He told us of that immense class who live in New York without a church-home, of the heathen that are growing up among us.

"You need not go to Africa," said he, "to find them. They come to your door every morning for cold victuals. God will hold you responsible for their souls. Are you in the Sabbath-school? Are you in the Mission-school? Are you in the neighborhood prayer-meeting? Are you a visitor? Are you distributing tracts? Are you doing anything to seek and to save that which is lost?" Then he went on to say what should be done; and to maintain the right and duty of laymen to preach, to teach, to visit, to do all things which belong to "fishers of men." "There are a great many church members," said he, "who seem to suppose that their whole duty consists in paying pew rent and listening to preaching. That is not Christianity. If you are doing nothing you are drones. There is no room in the hive for you. The Church has too many idle Christians already. We don't want you."

He did not argue. He simply asserted. But he evidently felt the truth of all that he said. I believe I should have decided at once to go into the Sabbath-school as soon as I came home, but for a little incident.

After church I walked home with Mr. Lane to dine with him. Mr. Sower joined and walked along with us. He is at the head of a large manufacturing establishment. He is one of Mr. Lane's warmest friends. Mr. Lane believes him to be a devoted Christian. "Well, parson," said he, "I suppose after to-night's sermon there is nothing left for me to do but to take a letter from the Church--if you don't excommunicate me before I get it."

"What's the matter now?" said the parson.

"I am neither visiting," said Mr. Sower, "nor distributing tracts, nor attending a tenement-house prayer-meeting, nor preaching, nor working in a mission, nor doing anything in the Church, but going to its service and paying my pew rent, and sometimes a little something over to make up a deficiency. The fact is every day in the week I have my breakfast an hour before you do, and am off to the factory. I never get home till six o'clock, sometimes not then. My day's work uses up my day's energies. I can't go out to a tenement-house prayer-meeting, or to tract distribution in the evening. I can hardly keep awake in our own church prayer-meeting. If it were not for Sunday's rest my work would kill me in a year. I sometimes think that perhaps I am devoting too much of my time to money-making. But what shall I do? There are four hundred workmen in the factory. Most of them have families. All of those families are really dependent on me for their daily bread. It takes all my life's energies to keep them employed. Shall I leave that work to take hold of tenement-house visitation and tract distribution?"

Mr. Lane replied promptly that Mr. Sower was to do no such thing. "Your factory," said he, "is your field. That is the work God has given you to do. It is your parish. Do not leave it for another--only do not forget that you have to give an account of your parochial charge. You are to study, not how to get the most money out of your four hundred workmen, but how to do them the most good. That is Christian duty for you. But your case is very peculiar. There is not one man in a thousand situated as you are."

Then I began to think that perhaps my law office was my field. It gives me enough to do I am sure. We are not all drones who are not working for the Church. There is a work for Christ outside. And I do not want to take a Sabbath-school class. I want Sunday mornings to myself. Every other morning I have to be an early riser. I do enjoy being lazy Sunday morning.

But then there is that class of young men from the mill. Deacon Goodsole says they don't know anything. He has no one who can manage them. And Mr. Work thinks it's a dreadful sin, I do not doubt, that I do not take it at once. I do not care much for that. But Jennie says I am just the one to manage these boys if I feel like undertaking it. And I would like to prove her good opinion of me true.

I was just in that perplexity when night before last a meeting on behalf of the City Mission Society was held here. Mr. Mingins, the Superintendent of city missions, was one of the speakers.

He made an earnest and at times a really eloquent speech. He would have made a splendid jury lawyer. He depicted in the most lively colors the wretched condition of the outcast population of New York. With all the eloquence of a warm heart, made more attractive by his broad Scotch, he pled with us to take an active part in their amelioration. "Pure religion and undefiled, before God and the Father, is this," cried he, "to visit the fatherless and widows in their affliction, and to keep himself unspotted from the world."

I resolved to take up that class of Mission boys straightways. But as I came out I met Hattie Bridgeman. She is an old friend of Jennie's and has had a hard, hard life. Her husband is an invalid. Her children are thrown on her for support. As I met her at the door she pressed my hand without speaking. I could see by the trembling lip and the tearful eye, that her heart was full. "I wish I had not come to-night," she said, as we walked along together. "Such stories make my heart bleed. It seems as though I ought to go right out to visit the sick, comfort the afflicted, care for the neglected. But what can I do? My children are dependent on me. These six weeks at Wheathedge are my only vacation. The rest of the time I am teaching music from Monday morning till Saturday night. Sunday, when I ought to rest, is my most exhausting day. For then I sing in church. If I were to leave my scholars my children would starve. How can I do anything for my Savior?"

It was very plain that she was to serve her Savior in the music lesson as indeed she does. For she goes into every house as a missionary. She carries the spirit of Christ in her heart. His joy is radiant in her face. She preaches the Gospel in houses where neighborhood prayer-meetings cannot be held, in households which tract-distributors never enter. The street that needs Gospel visitation most is Fifth avenue. That is in her district. And, nobly, though unconsciously, she fulfils her mission. More than one person I have heard say, "If to be a Christian is to be like Mrs. Bridgeman, I wish I were one." Our pastor preaches no such effective sermons as does she by her gentleness, her geniality, her patience, her long suffering with joyfulness. And when the Sabbath comes, her voice, though it leads the service of song in a fashionable city church, expresses the ardor of her Christian heart, and is fraught with quite as true devotion as the prayers of her pastor.

Something like this Jennie told her as we walked along from church; and she left us comforted. And I was a little comforted too. It is very clear, is it not, that we are not all drones who are not at work in the church. There are other fields than the Sabbath-school.

Do I carry Christ into my law office, and into the court-room, as Mrs. Bridgeman does into the parlor and the chair? That is the first point to be settled. The other comes up afterward. But it does persist in coming up. It is not settled yet. Will it hurt my Sunday to take that class for an hour? I doubt it.

I must talk it over with Jennie and see what she really thinks about it.

CHAPTER VII.
The Field is the World.

LAST evening before I had found an opportunity to talk it over with Jennie, Dr. Argure and Deacon Goodsole called. I suspect the deacon's conscience had been quickened even more than mine respecting my duty to that mission class by Mr. Minging's address. For I have noticed that our consciences are apt to be quickened by sermons and addresses more respecting our neighbors' duties even than respecting our own.

Dr. Argure had come down the day before from Newtown to attend the city mission meeting. He is a very learned man. At least I suppose he is, for everybody says so. He is at all events a very sonorous man. He has a large vocabulary of large words, and there are a great many people who cannot distinguish between great words and great thoughts. I do not mean to impugn his intellectual capital when I say that he does a very large credit business. In sailing on lake Superior you can sometimes see the rocky bottom 30 or 40 feet below the surface--the water is so clear. You never can see the bottom of Dr. Argure's sermons. Perhaps it is because they are so deep; I sometimes think it is because they are so muddy. Still he really is an able man, and knows the books, and knows how to turn his knowledge to a good account. Last summer he preached a sermon at Wheathedge, on female education. He told us about female education among the Greeks, and the Romans, and the Hebrews, and the Persians, and the Egyptians--though not much about it in America of to-day. But it was a learned discourse--at least I suppose so. Three weeks after, I met the President of the Board of Trustees of the Polltown Female Seminary, I mentioned incidentally that I was spending the summer at Wheathedge.

"You have got a strong man up there somewhere," said he, "that Dr. Argure, of Newtown. He delivered an address before our seminary last week on female education; full of learning sir, full of learning. We put him right on our Board of Trustees. Next year I think we shall make him President."

A month or so after I found in the weekly Watch Tower an editorial,--indeed I think there were three in successive numbers--on female education. They had a familiar sound, and happening to meet the editor, I spoke of them.

"Yes," said he "they are by Dr. Argure. A very learned man that sir. Does an immense amount of work too. He is one of our editorial contributors as perhaps you see, and an able man, very learned sir. Those are very original and able articles sir."

This fall I took up the Adriatic Magazine, and there what should my eye fall on but an article on female education. I did not read it; but the papers assured their readers that it was a learned and exhaustive discussion on the whole subject by that scholarly and erudite writer, Dr. Argure. And having heard this asserted so often, I began to think that it certainly must be true. And then in January I received a pamphlet on female education by Dr. Argure. It was addressed to the Board of Education, and demanded a higher course of training for woman, and was a learned and exhaustive discussion of the whole subject from the days of Moses down.

"An able man that Dr. Argure," said Mr. Wheaton to me the other day referring to that same pamphlet.

"Yes, I think he is," I could not help saying. "I think he can stir more puddings with one pudding stick than any other man I know."

Still he stirs them pretty well. And if he can do it I do not know that there is any objection.

But if I do not believe in Dr. Argure quite as fully as some less sceptical members of his congregation do, Deacon Goodsole believes in him most implicitly. Deacon Goodsole is a believer--not I mean in anything in particular, but generally. He likes to believe; he enjoys it; he does it, not on evidence, but on general principles. The deacons of the stories are all crabbed, gnarled, and cross-grained. They are the terrors of the little boys, and the thorn in the flesh to the minister. But Deacon Goodsole is the most cheery, bright, and genial of men. He is like a streak of sunshine. He sensibly radiates the prayer-meeting, which would be rather cold except for him. The little boys always greet him with a "How do you do Deacon," and always get a smile, and a nod, and sometimes a stick of candy or a little book in return. His overcoat pockets are always full of some little books or tracts, and always of the bright and cheery description. Always full, I said; but that is a mistake; when he gets home at night they are generally empty. For he goes out literally as a sower went out to sow, I do not believe there is a child within five miles of Wheathedge that has not had one of the Deacon's little books.

I suspected that the Deacon had come partly to talk with me about that Bible class, and I resolved to give him an opportunity. So I opened the way at once.

Laicus.:

--Well Deacon, how are church affairs coining on; pretty smoothly; salary paid up at last?

Deacon Goodsole.:

--Yes, Mr. Laicus; and we're obliged to you for it too. I don't think the parson would have got his money but for you.

Laicus.:

--Not at all, Deacon. Thank my wife, not me. She was righteously indignant at the church for leaving its minister unpaid so long. If I were the parson I would clear out that Board of Trustees and put in a new one, made up wholly of women.

Deacon Goodsole.:

--That's not a bad idea. I believe the women would make a deal better Board than the present one.

Dr. Argure: [(with great solemnity).]

--Mr. Laicus, have you considered the Scriptural teachings concerning the true relations and sphere of women in the church of Christ. The apostle says very distinctly that he does not suffer a woman to teach or to usurp authority over the man, and it is very clear that to permit the female members of the church to occupy such offices as those you have indicated would be to suffer her to usurp that authority which the Scripture reposes alone in the head--that is in man.

Laicus: [(naively).]

--Does the Scripture really say that women must not teach?

Dr. Argure.:

--Most certainly it does, sir. The apostle is very explicit on that point, very explicit. And I hold, sir, that for women to preach, or to speak in public, or in the prayer-meeting of the church, is a direct violation of the plain precepts of the inspired word.

Laicus.:

--I wonder you have any women teach in your Sabbath School? Or have you turned them all out?

Mrs. Laicus,: [(who evidently wishes to change the conversation).]

--How do affairs go on in the work of your church.

Dr. Argure,: [(who is not unwilling that it should be changed).]

--But slowly, madam. There is not that readiness and zeal in the work of the church, which I would wish to see. There are many fruitless branches on the tree, Mrs. Laicus, many members of my church who do nothing really to promote its interests. They are not to be found in the Sabbath School; they cannot be induced to participate actively in tract distribution; and they are even not to be depended on in the devotional week-day meetings of the church.

Deacon Goodsole,: [(who always goes straight to the point).]

--Mr. Laicus here needs a little touching up on that point, Doctor; and I am glad you are here to do it. How as to that Bible class, Mr. Laicus, that I spoke to you about week before last? There are four or five young men from the barrow factory in the Sabbath School now. But they have no teacher. I am sure if you could see your way clear to take that class you would very soon have as many more. There are some thirty of them that rarely or never come to church. And as for me, I can't get at them. They are mostly unbelievers. Mr. Gear himself, the superintendent, is a regular out and out infidel. And I never could do anything with unbelievers

Laicus.:

--Deacon, I wish I could. But I am very busy all through the week, and I really don't see how I can take this work up on Sunday. Beside it would require some week-day work in addition.

Dr. Argure.:

--No man can be too busy to serve the Lord, Mr. Laicus; certainly no professed disciple of the Lord. The work of the church, Mr. Laicus, is before every other work in its transcendant importance.

Laicus.:

--I don't know about that. Seems to me, I have seen somewhere that if a man does not provide for his own family he is worse than an infidel.

Dr. Argure,: [(putting this response away from him majestically).]

--It is unfortunately too common an excuse even with professors of religion that they are too busy to serve in the work of the Lord. There is for example the instance of Dr. Curall. He was elected at my suggestion last summer as an elder in our church. But he declined the office, which the apostle declares to be honorable, and of such a character that if it be well used they who employ it purchase to themselves a good degree. Alas! that it should be so frequently so-- ourselves first and Christ afterwards.

Laicus.:

--Is that quite fair Dr? Must Dr. Curall be put down as refusing to follow the Master because he refuses to leave the duties of his profession which he is doing well, to take on those of a church office which he might do but poorly? May not he who goes about healing the sick be following Christ as truly as he who preaches the Gospel to the poor? Is the one to be accused of serving the world any more because of his fees than the other because of his salary? Can an elder do any more to carry the Gospel of Christ to the sick bed and the house of mourning than a Christian physician, if he is faithful as a Christian?

Dr. Argure shook his head but made no response.

Deacon Goodsole.:

--That may do very well in the case of a doctor, Mr. Laicus. But I don't see how it applies in your case, or in that of farmer Faragon, or in that of Typsel the printer or in that of Sole the boot-maker, or in that of half a score of people I could name, who are doing nothing in the church except pay their pew rent.

Laicus.:

--Suppose you pass my case for the moment, and take the others. Take farmer Faragon for example. He has a farm of three hundred acres. It keeps him busy all the week. He works hard, out of doors, all day. When evening comes he gets his newspaper, sits down by the fire and pretends to read. But I have noticed that he rarely reads ten minutes before he drops asleep. When he comes to church the same phenomenon occurs. He cannot resist the soporific tendencies of the furnaces. By the time Mr. Work gets fairly into secondly, Farmer Faragon is sound asleep. So he does not even listen to the preaching. Is he then a drone? Suppose you make a calculation how many mouths he feeds indirectly by the products of his farm. I cannot even guess. But I know nothing ever goes from it that is not good. The child is happy that drinks his milk, the butcher fortunate who buys his beef, the housewife well off who has his apples and potatoes in her cellar. He never sends a doubtful article to market; never a short weight or a poor measure. I think that almost every one who deals with him recognizes in him a Christian man. He does not work in Sunday School, it is true, but he has brought more than one farm hand into it. Christ fed five thousand by the sea of Galilee with five loaves and two small fishes. Was that Christian? Farmer Faragon, feeds, in his small way, by his industry, a few scores of hungry mortals. Is he a drone?

Or take Mr. Typsel the printer. He publishes the Newtown Chronicle. He sends a weekly message to 10,000 readers, at least twenty times as many as Dr. Argure's congregation. I do not know how good a Christian he is; I do not know much about the Newtown Chronicle. But I know that the press is exerting an incalculable influence over the people, for good or for ill and the man who devotes his energies to it, and really uses it to educate and elevate the community, is doing as much in his sphere for Christ as the minister in his. He has no right to neglect the greater work God has given him to do for the lesser work of teaching a Sabbath School class.

Jennie.:

--That is if he cannot well do both.

Laicus.:

--Yes--of course. If he can do both, that is very well.

Dr. Argure.:

--That's a very dangerous doctrine Mr. Laicus.

Laicus,: [(warmly).]

--If it is true it is not dangerous. The truth is never dangerous.

Dr. Argure.:

--The truth is not to be spoken at all times.

Deacon Goodsole.:

--That's a very unnecessary doctrine, Dr., to teach to a lawyer.

Dr. Argure,: [(indifferent alike to the sally and to the laugh which follows it).]

--Consider, Mr. Laicus, what would be the effect on the church of preaching that doctrine. It is our duty to build up the church. It is the church which is the pillar and ground of the truth. It is the church which is Christ's great instrumentality for the conversion of the world. When the kingdoms of this world become the kingdoms of our Lord and of his Christ, then the church will have universal dominion. Here in Wheathedge, for example, Mr. Work is laboring to build up and strengthen the church of Christ. And you tell his people and the people of hundreds of similar parishes all over the land, that it is no matter whether they do any work in the church or not. Consider the effect of it.

Laicus.:

--It seems to me, Dr., that you entertain a low, though a very common, conception of your office. The ministers are not mere builders of churches. They are set to build men. The church which will have universal dominion is not this or that particular organization, but the whole body of those who love the truth as it is in Christ Jesus. Churches, creeds, covenants, synods, assemblies, associations, will all fade; the soul alone is immortal. If you are really building for eternity you cannot merely build churches.

Dr. Argure.:

--Consider then, Mr. Laicus, the effect of your doctrine on the hearts and souls of men. Consider how many idle and indifferent professors of religion there are, who are doing nothing in the church, and nothing for the church. And you tell them that it is just as well they should not; that they are just as worthy of honor as if they were active in the Lords vineyard?

Laicus.:

--It is just as well if they are really serving Christ. It does not make any difference whether they are doing it in the church or out of the church. Christ himself served chiefly out of the church, and had it arrayed against him. So did Paul; so did Luther.

Deacon Goodsole.:

--Do you mean that it makes no difference, Mr. Laicus, whether a man is a member of the church or not?

Laicus.:

--Not at all. That is quite another matter. I am speaking of church work, not of church membership; and I insist that church work and Christian work are not necessarily synonymous. I insist that whatever tends to make mankind better, nobler, wiser, permanently happier, if it is work carried on in the spirit of Christ is work for Christ, whether it is done in the church or out of the church. I insist that every layman is bound to do ten-fold more for Christ out of the church than in its appointed ways and under its supervision. I have read, Dr., with a great deal of interest your learned and exhaustive treatise on the higher education of women, (I am afraid I told a little lie there; but had not the Dr. just told me that the truth was not to be told at all times), but I declare to you, that so far as the elevation of woman is concerned, I would rather have invented the sewing machine than have been the author of all the sermons, addresses, magazine articles, editorials and pamphlets on the woman question that have been composed since Paul wrote his second Epistle to the Christians.

Dr. Argure,: [(shaking his head).]

--It is a dangerous doctrine, Mr. Laicus, a dangerous doctrine. You do not consider its effect on the minds of the common people.

Laicus,: [(thoroughly aroused and thoroughly in earnest).]

--Do you consider the influence of the opposite teaching, both on the church and on the individual? We are building churches, you tell us. The "outsiders," as we call them, very soon understand that. They see that we are on the look-out for men who can build us up, not for men whom we can build up. If a wealthy man comes into the neighborhood, we angle for him. If a devout, active, praying Christian moves into the neighborhood, we angle for him. If a drunken loafer drops down upon us, does anybody ever angle for him? If a poor, forlorn widow, who has to work from Monday morning till Saturday night, comes to dwell under the shadow

of our church, do we angle for her? Yes! I am glad to believe we do. But the shrewdness, the energy, the tact, is displayed in the other kind of fishing. Don't you suppose "the world" understand this? Don't you suppose our Mr. Wheaton understands
what we want him in the board of trustees for? Such men interpret our invitation-
-and they are not very wrong--as, come with us and do us good; not, come with us
and we will do you good.

Consider, too, its effect on the individual. I attended a morning prayer meeting
last winter in the city. A young man told his experience. He started in the morning, he said, to go to the store. But it seemed as though the Lord bid him retrace his
steps. A voice within seemed to say to him, "Your duty is at the prayer meeting."
The battle between Christ and the world was long and bitter. Christ at length pre-
vailed. He had come to the prayer meeting. He wanted to tell the brethren what
Christ had done for his soul. The experience may have been genuine. It may have
been his duty to leave the store for the church that particular morning. But what is
the effect of a training which teaches a young man to consider all the time he gives
to the store as time appropriated to the world? It is that he can serve both God and
mammon; that he actually does. It draws a sharp line between the sacred and secular. And most of his life is necessarily the secular.

I forgot to mention that Mrs. Goodsole had come over with her husband. She
and Jennie sat side by side. But she had not opened her mouth since the salutations
of the evening had been interchanged. She is the meekest and mildest of women.
She is also the most timed. In public she rarely speaks. But it is currently reported
that she avenges herself for her silence by the curtain lectures, she delivers to her
good husband at home. Of that, however, I cannot be sure. I speak only of rumor.
Now she took advantage of a pause to say:

Mrs. Goodsole.:

--I like Mr. Laicus's doctrine. It's very comforting to a woman like me who am
so busy at home that I can hardly get out to church on Sundays.

Deacon Goodsole.:

--I don't believe it's true. Yes I do too. But I don't believe it's applicable. That
is--well what I mean to say--I can't express myself exactly, but my idea is this, that
the people that won't work in the church are the very ones that do nothing out of it.
The busy ones are busy everywhere. There is Mr. Line, for example. He has a large

farm. He keeps a summer hotel, two houses always full; and they are capitally kept houses. That, of itself, is enough to keep any man busy. The whole burden of both hotel and farm rests on his shoulders. And yet he is elder and member of the board of trustees, and on hand, in every kind of exigency, in the church. He is one of the public school commissioners, is active in getting new roads laid out, and public improvements introduced, is the real founder of our new academy, and, in short, has a hand in every good work that is ever undertaken in Wheathedge. And there is Dr. Curall, whose case Mr. Laicus has advocated so eloquently and who is too busy to be an elder; and I verily believe I could count all his patients on the fingers of my two hands.

Mrs. Goodsole,: [(inclined to agree with everybody, and so to live at peace and amity with all mankind).]

--There is something in that. There is Mrs. Wheaton who has only one child, a grown up boy, and who keeps three or four servants to take care of herself and her husband and her solitary son, and she is always too busy to do anything in the church.

Deacon Goodsole.:

--On the other hand there is not a busier person in the church than Miss Moore. She supports herself and her widowed mother by teaching. She is in school from nine till three, and gives private lessons three evenings in the week, and yet she finds time to visit all the sick in the neighborhood. And when last year we held a fair to raise money for an organ for the Sabbath school, she was the most active and indefatigable worker among them all. Mrs. Bisket was the only one who compared with her. And Mrs. Bisket keeps a summer boarding-house, and it was the height of the season, and she only had one girl part of the time.

Dr. Argure rose to go, Deacon Goodsole followed his example. There were a few minutes of miscellaneous conversation as the gentlemen put on their coats. As we followed them to the library door Deacon Goodsole turned to me:--

"But you have not given me your answer yet, Mr. Laicus," said he.

Before I could give it, Jennie had drawn her arm through mine, and looking up into my face for assent had answered for me. "He will think of it, Mr. Goodsole," said she. "He never decides any question of importance without sleeping on it."

I have been thinking of it. I am sure that I am right in my belief that there are many ways of working for Christ beside working for the church. I am sure the first thing is for us to work for Christ in our daily, secular affairs. I am sure that all are not drones who are not buzzing in the ecclesiastical hive. But I am not so sure that I have not time to take that Bible-class. I am not so sure that the busy ones in the church are not also the busy ones out of the church. I remember that when Mr. James Harper was hard at work establishing the business of Harper & Brothers, which has grown to such immense proportions since, at the very time he was work-ing night as well as day to expedite publications, he was a trustee and class-leader in John Street Methodist Church, and rarely missed the sessions of the board or the meetings of the class. I remember that Mr. Hatch, the famous banker, was almost the founder of the Jersey City Tabernacle Church, and his now President of the Howard Mission. Yet I suppose there is not a busier man in Wall street. I remember that Wm. E. Dodge, jr., and Morris K. Jessup, than whom there are few men more industrious, commercially, are yet both active in City Missions and in the Young Men's Christian Association; the former is an elder in an up-town church, and very active in Sabbath School work. I remember Ralph Wells, bishop of all the Presby-terian Sabbath Schools for miles around New York, who was, until lately, active in daily business in the city. Yes I am sure that hard work in the week is not always a good reason for refusing to work in the church on the Sabbath.

"Jennie, I am going to try that Bible class, as an experiment, for the winter."

"I am glad of it, John."

CHAPTER VIII.
Mr. Gear.

"JENNIE," said I, "Harry and I are going out for our walk."

It was Sunday afternoon. I had enjoyed my usual Sunday afternoon nap, and now I was going out for my usual Sunday afternoon walk. Only this afternoon I had a purpose beside that of an hour's exercise in the fresh air.

"I wish I could go with you John," said Jennie, "but it's Fanny's afternoon out, and I can't leave the baby. Where are you going?"

"Up to the mill village, to see Mr. Gear," said I. "I am going to ask him to join the Bible class."

"Why John he's an infidel I thought."

"So they say," I replied. "But it can't do an infidel any harm to study the Bible. I may not succeed; I probably shan't; but I certainly shan't if I don't try."

"I wish I could do something to help you John. And I think I can. I can pray for you. Perhaps that will help you?"

Help me. With the assurance of those prayers I walked along the road with a new confidence of hope. Before I had dreaded my errand, now I was in haste for the interview. I believe in the intercession of the saints; and Jennie is a--but I forget. The public are rarely interested in a man's opinion about his own wife.

The mill village, as we call it, is a little collection of cottages with one or two houses of a somewhat more pretentious character, which gather round the wheel-barrow factory down the river, a good mile's walk from the church. It was a bright afternoon in October. The woods were in the glory of their radiant death, the air was crisp and keen. Harry who now ran before, now loitered behind, and now walked sedately by my side, was full of spirits, and there was everything to make the soul feel hope and courage. And yet I had my misgivings. When I had told Deacon Goodsole that I was going to call on Mr. Gear he exclaimed at my proposition.

"Why he's a regular out and outer. He does not believe in anything--Church, Bible, Sunday, Christ, God or even his own immortality."

"What do you know of him?" I asked.

"He was born in New England," replied the Deacon, "brought up in an orthodox family, taught to say the Westminster Assembly's Catechism (he can say it better than I can today), and listened twice every Sunday till he was eighteen to good sound orthodox preaching. Then he left home and the church together; and he has never been to either, to remain, since."

"Does he ever go to church?" I asked.

The Deacon shrugged his shoulders. "I asked him that question myself the other day," said he. "You never go to church, Mr. Gear, I believe?" said I.

"Oh! yes I do," he replied. "I go home every Christmas to spend a week. And at home I always go to church for the sake of the old folks. At Wheathedge I always stay away for my own sake."

"And what do you know of his theology?" said I.

"Theology," said the Deacon; "he hasn't any. His creed is the shortest and sim-plest one I know of. I tried to have a religious conversation with him once but I had to give it up. I could make nothing out of him. He said he believed in the existence of a God. But he scouted the idea that we could know anything about Him. He was rather inclined to think there was a future life; but nobody knew anything about it. All that we could know was that if we are virtuous in this life we shall be happy in the next--if there is a next."

"He does not believe that the gates are wide open there," said I.

"No," said the Deacon; "nor ajar either."

"And what does he say of Christ and Christianity," said I.

"Of Jesus Christ," said the Deacon, "that--well--probably such a man lived, and was a very pure and holy man, and a very remarkable teacher, certainly for his age a very remarkable teacher. But he ridicules the idea of the miracles; says he does not believe them any more than he believes in the mythical legends of Greek and Roman literature. And as to Christianity he believes its a very good sort of thing, better for America than any other religion; but he rather thinks Buddhism is very likely better for India."

"But I wish you would go and see him," continued the Deacon. "Perhaps you can make something out of him. I can't. I have tried again and again, and I always get the worst of it. He is well read, I assure you, and keen as--as," the Deacon failed in his search for a simile and closed his sentence with--"a great deal keener than I am. He's a real good fellow, but he doesn't believe in anything. There is no use in quoting Scripture, because he thinks it's nothing but a collection of old legends. I once tried to argue the question of inspiration with him. 'Deacon,' said he to me, 'suppose a father should start off one fine morning to carry his son up to the top of Hurricane Hill and put him to death there, and should pretend he had a revela-tion from God to do it, what would you do to him?' 'Put him in the insane asylum,' said I. 'Exactly,' said he. 'My boys came home from your Sabbath School the other Sunday full of the sacrifice of Isaac, and Will, who takes after his father, asked me if I didn't think it was cruel for God to tell a father to kill his own son. What could I say? I don't often interfere, because it troubles my wife so. But I couldn't stand that, and I told him very frankly that I didn't believe the story, and if it was true I thought Abraham was crazy.' He had me there, you know," continued the Deacon, good- naturedly, "but then I never was good for anything in discussion. I wish you would go to see him, may be you would bring him to terms."

And so I was going now, not without misgivings, and with no great faith in any capacity on my part to "bring him to terms," as the Deacon phrased it, but buoyed up a good deal, notwithstanding, by the remembrance of those promised prayers.

And yet though Mr. Gear is an infidel he is not a bad man. Even Dr. Argure, and he is fearfully sound on the doctrine of total depravity, admits that there are some good traits about him, "natural virtues" he is careful to explain, not "saving graces."

Of his thorough, incorruptible honesty, no man ever intimated a doubt. In every business transaction he is the soul of honor. His word is a great deal better than Jim Wheaton's bond.

In every good work he is a leader. When the new school-house was to be built, Mr. Gear was put, by an almost unanimous consent, upon the Board, and made its treasurer. When, last Fall, rumors were rife of the mismanagement of the Poor-house, Mr. Gear was the one to demand an investigation, and, being put upon the Committee, to push through against a good deal of opposition, till he secured the reform that was needed. In his shop there is not a man whose personal history he does not know, not one who does not count him a personal friend. That there has not been a strike for ten years is due to the workmen's personal faith in him. When Robert Dale was caught in the shafting and killed last winter, it was Mr. Gear who paid the widow's rent out of his own pocket, got the eldest son a place on a farm, and carried around personally a subscription to provide for the family, after starting it handsomely himself. He is appointed to arbitrate in half the incipient quarrels of the neighborhood, and settles more controversies, I am confident, than his neighbor, Squire Hodgson, though the latter is a Justice of the Peace. There is always difficulty in collecting our pew rents. Half the church members are from one week to one quarter behind-hand. Mr. Gear has a pew for his family, and his pew-rent is always paid before it becomes due. The Deacon tells me confidentially, that Mr. Work does not think it prudent to preach against intemperance because Jim Wheaton always has wine on his table New Year's day. Mr. Gear is the head of the Good Templars, and has done more to circulate the pledge among the workmen of the town than all the rest of us put together. He is naturally an intensely passionate man, and I am told rips out an oath now and then. But that he is vigorously laboring with himself to control his temper is very evident, and it is equally evident, so at least the Deacon says, that he is gaining a victory in this life-campaign.

"It is very clear," said I to myself, as I walked along, "that there are some good points in Mr. Gear's character. He must have a side where Christian truth could get in, if one could only find it; where indeed it does get in, though he thinks, and every one else thinks, it does not. Be it my task to find the place."

CHAPTER IX.
I get my first Bible Scholar.

A pretty little cottage-white, with green blinds; the neatest of neat fences; a little platform in front of the sidewalk with three steps leading up to it,--a convenient method of access to our high country carriages; two posts before the gate neatly turned, a trellis over the front door with a climbing rose which has mounted half way to the top and stopped to rest for the season; another trellis fan-shaped behind which a path disappears that leads round to the kitchen door; the tastiest of little bird houses, now tenantless and desolate,--this is the picture that meets my eye and assures me that Mr. Gear is a man both of taste and thrift, as indeed he is.

Mrs. Gear who comes to the door in answer to my knock and who is a cheerful little body with yet a tinge of sadness in her countenance, as one who knows some secret sorrow which her blithe heart cannot wholly sing away, is very glad to see me. She calls me by my name and introduces herself with a grace that is as much more graceful as it is more natural than the polished and stately manners which Mrs. Wheaton has brought with her from fashionable society to Wheathedge. Mr. Gear is out, he has gone down to the shop,--will I walk in,--he will be back directly. I am very happy to walk in, and Mrs. Gear introducing me to a cozy little sitting-room with a library table in the centre, and a book-case on one side, well filled too, takes Harry by the hand, and leads him out to introduce him to the great Newfoundland dog whom we saw basking in the sunshine on the steps of the side door, as we came up the road.

I am accustomed to judge of men by their companions, and books are companions. So whenever I am in a parlor alone I always examine the book-case. or the centre table--if there is one. In Mrs. Wheaton's parlor I find no book-case, but a large centre table on which there are several annuals with a great deal of gilt binding and very little reading, and a volume or two of plates, sometimes handsome, more often showy. In the library, which opens out of the parlor, I find sets of the classic authors in library bindings, but when I take one down it betrays the fact that no other hand has touched it to open it before. And I know that Jim Wheaton buys books to furnish his house, just as he buys wall paper and carpets. At Mr. Hardcap's I find a big family Bible, and half a dozen of those made up volumes fat with thick paper and large type, and showy with poor pictures, which constitute the common literature of two thirds of our country homes. And I know that poor Mr. Hardcap is the unfortunate victim of book agents. At Deacon Goodsole's I always see some school books lying in admirable confusion on the sitting-room table. And I know that Deacon Goodsole has children, and that they bring their books home at night to do some real studying, and that they do it in the family sitting-room and get help now and then from father and from mother. And so while I am waiting for Mr. Gear I take a furtive glance at his well filled shelves. I am rather surprized to find in his little library so large a religious element, though nearly all of it heterodox. There is a complete edition of Theodore Parker's works, Channing's works, a volume or two of Robertson, one of Furness. the English translation of Strauss' Life of Christ, Renan's Jesus, and half a dozen more similar books, intermingled with volumes of history, biography, science, travels, and the New American Cyclopedia. The Radical and the Atlantic Monthly are on the table. The only orthodox book is Beecher's Sermons,--and I believe Dr. Argure says they are not orthodox; the only approach to fiction is one of Oliver Wendell Holmes' books, I do not now remember which one. "Well," said I to myself, "whatever this man is, he is not irreligious."

I had just arrived at this conclusion when Mr. Gear entered. A tall, thin, nervous man, with a high forehead, piercing black eyes, and a restless uneasiness that forbids him from ever being for a moment still. Now he runs his hand through his hair pushing it still further back from his dome of a head, now he drums the table with his uneasy fingers, now he crosses and uncrosses his long legs, and once, as our conversation grows animated, he rises from his seat in the vehemence of his earnestness, and leans against the mantel piece. A clear-eyed, frank faced, fine looking man, who would compel your heed if you met him anywhere, unknown, by chance, on the public street. "An infidel you may be," I say to myself, "but not a bad man; on the contrary a man with much that is true and noble, or I am no physiognomist or phrenologist either." And I rather pride myself on being both.

We lawyers learn to study the faces of our witnesses, to form quick judgments, and to act upon them. If I did not mistake my man the directest method was the best, and I employed it.

"Mr. Gear," said I, "I have come to ask you to join my Bible class."

"Me!" said Mr. Gear unmistakeably surprised. "I don't believe in the Bible."

"So I have heard," I said quietly. "And that's the reason I came to you first. In fact I do not want you to join my Bible class. I have not got any Bible class as yet, I want you to join me in getting one up."

Mr. Gear smiled incredulously. "You had better get Deacon Goodsole," said he,--"or," and the smile changed from a goodnatured to a sarcastic one, "or Mr. Hardcap."

"I have no doubt they would either of them join me," said I. "But they believe substantially as I have been taught to believe about the Bible. They have learned to look at it through creeds, and catechisms, and orthodox preaching. I want to get a fresh look at it. I want to come to it as I would come to any other book, and to find out what it means, not what it seems to mean to a man who has been bred to believe that it is only the flesh and blood of which the dry bones are the Westminster Assembly's Catechism."

"Mr. Laicus," said Mr. Gear, "I thank you for the honor you do me. But I don't believe in the Bible. I don't believe it's the word of God any more than Homer or Tacitus. I don't believe those old Hebrews knew any more than we do--nor half so much. It says the world was made in six days. I think it more likely it was six millions of years in making."

"So do I," said I.

"It says God rested on the Sabbath day. I believe He always works, day and night, summer and winter, in every blazing fire, in every gathering storm, in every rushing river, in every growing flower, in every falling leaf."

He rose as he spoke and stood, now leaning against the mantel piece, now standing erect, his dark eyes flashing, his great forehead seeming to expand with great thoughts, his soul all enkindled with his own eloquence: for eloquent he really was, and all unconscious of it.

"Your Bible," said he "shuts God up in a Temple, and in an ark in that, and hides him behind curtains where the High priest can find him but once a year. My God is every where. There is no church that can hold him. The heavens are his home; the earth is his footstool. All this bright and beautiful world is his temple. He is in every mountain, in every cloud, in every winter wind and every summer breeze."

He looked so handsome in his earnest eloquence that I had no heart to interrupt him. And yet I waited and watched for any opening he might give me, and thought of Jennie, and her prayers at home, and declared to myself by God's help I would not let this man go till I had caught him and brought him to know the love that now he knew not.

"Your Bible, Mr. Laicus," said he, "sets apart one day for the Lord and gives all the rest to the world, the flesh, and the devil. I believe all days are divine, all days are the Lord's, all hours are sacred hours and all ground is holy ground."

I wanted to tell him that my Bible did no such thing. But I had fully considered what I would do before I had sought this interview. I had resolved that nothing should tempt me into a contradiction or an argument. I had studied Jennie's method, and I reserved my fire.

"Your Bible tells me," said he, "that God wrote his laws with his finger on two tables of stone; that he tried to preserve them from destruction by bidding them be kept in a sacred ark; and that despite his care they were broken in pieces before Moses got down from the mountain top. I believe he writes them impartially in nature and in our hearts, that science interprets them, and that no Moses astonished out of his presence of mind can harm them or break the tablets on which they are engraven."

So true, yet oh so false. Oh God! help me to teach him what my Bible really is and what its glorious teachings are.

"I don't believe the Bible is the Word of God. I can't believe it. I don't believe the laws of Moses are any more inspired than the laws of Solon, or the books of Samuel and Kings than the history of Tacitus, or the Psalms of David than the Paradise Lost of Milton, or--you'll think me bold indeed to say so Mr. Laicus," (he was cooler now and spoke more slowly), "the words of Jesus, than the precepts of

Confucius or the dialogues of Plato."

In that sentence he gave to me my clue. I seized it instantly, and never lost it from that moment. Never case in court so thrilled me with excitement as I too arose and leaned against the mantel-piece. And never was I, in tone and manner, calmer.

"As much so?" I asked carelessly.

"Yes....." said he, hesitatingly, "yes..... as much so I suppose."

"The ten commandments have been before the world for over three thousand years," said I. "The number that have learned them and accepted them as a guide, and found in them a practical help is to be counted by millions. There is hardly a child in Wheathedge that does not know something of them, and has not been made better for them; and hardly a man who knows Solon even by name. We can hardly doubt that the one is as well worth studying as the other, Mr. Gear."

"No," said Mr. Gear. "I don't deny that they are worth studying. But I do deny that they are inspired."

"The Psalms of David have supplied the Christian church with its best psalmody for nearly three thousand years," continued I. "They constitute the reservoir from which Luther, and Watts, and Wesley, and Doddridge, and a host of other singers have drawn their inspiration, and in which myriads untold have found the expression of their highest and holiest experiences, myriads who never heard of Homer. They are surely as well worth studying as his noble epics."

"I don't deny, they are worth studying," said Mr. Gear. "I only assert that they ought to be studied as any other books of noble thoughts, intermingled with grossest errors, should be studied."

"The words of Jesus," I continued more slowly than before "have changed the life and character of more than half the world, that half which alone possesses modern civilization, that half with which you and I, Mr. Gear, are most concerned. There was wonderful power in the doctrines of Buddha. But Buddhism has relapsed everywhere into the grossest of idolatries. There is a wonderful wealth of moral truth in the ethics of Confucius. But the ethics of Confucius have not saved the Chinese nation from stagnation and death. There is wonderful life-awaking power in the writings of Plato. But they are hid from the common people in a dead language, and when a Prof. Jowett gives them glorious resurrection in our vernacular, they are still hid from the common people by their subtlety. Every philosopher ought to study Plato. Every scholar may profitably study Buddha and Confucius. But every intelligent American ought to study the life and words of Jesus of Nazareth."

"I do," said Mr. Gear. "I do not disesteem Jesus of Nazareth. I honor him as first among men. I revere his noble life, his sublime death, and his incomparable teachings. I have read his life in the Gospels; I have read it as Strauss gives it; and as Renan gives it; and now I am devoting my Sunday afternoons to reading it as Pressense gives it. You see I am an impartial student. I read all sides."

"You think Christ's life and teaching worth your study then?" I said inquiringly.

"Worth my study? Of course I do," said he. "I am an infidel, Mr. Laicus; at least people commonly call me so, and think it very dreadful. But I do not mean to be ignorant of the Bible or of Christianity as Jesus Christ gave it to us. It needs winnowing. We have grown wiser and know better about many things since then. But it is well worth the studying and will be for many years to come."

"All I ask of you," said I, "is to let me to study it with you."

He made no answer; but looked me steadily in the eye as if to try and fathom some occult design.

"No," said I, "that is not all. As I came by Joe Poole's I saw half a dozen of the men from your shop lounging about the door. They could spend the afternoon to better purpose, Mr. Gear, in studying the life and words of Jesus."

"I know they could," he said. "No man can say that any word or influence of mine helped carry them to Joe Poole's bar."

"Will you lend your word and influence with mine to summon them away?" said I.

He made no answer.

"I saw a dozen others engaged at a game of ball upon the green as I passed by."

"A harmless sport, Mr. Laicus, and as well done on Sunday as on any other holiday."

"Perhaps," said I. "But an hour and a half from their Sunday in studying the life and words of Jesus would do them no harm, and detract nothing from their holiday. They do not study so hard throughout the week that the brain labor would be injurious."

Mr. Gear smiled.

"There is not a man in your shop, Mr. Gear, that would not be made a better workman, husband, father, citizen, for studying that life and those teachings one hour a week."

"It is true," said he.

"You organized a Shakspeare club last winter to keep them from Joe Poole's," said I. "Was it a good thing?"

"Worked capitally," said Mr. Gear.

"Won't you join me in organizing a Bible club for Sunday afternoons this winter for the same purpose?"

"There is so little in common between us," said he; and he looked me through and through with his sharp black eyes. What a lawyer he would have made; what a cross examination he could conduct.

"You believe in the literal inspiration of the New Testament Scripture. I believe it is a book half legend half history. You believe in the miracles. I believe they are mythical addition of a later date. You believe that Jesus Christ was conceived of the Holy Ghost and born of the Virgin Mary. I believe his birth was as natural as his death was cruel and untimely. You believe that--he was divine. I believe he was a man of like passions as we ourselves are,--a Son of God only as every noble spirit is a spark struck off from the heavenly Original. You believe that he bears our sins upon a tree. I believe that every soul must bear its own burdens. What is there in common between us? What good could it do to you or to me to take Sunday afternoon for a weekly tournament, with the young men from the shop for arbitrators?"

"None," said I calmly.

"What would you have then?" said he.

"When you organized that Shakspeare club last winter," said I, "did you occupy your time in discussions of the text? Did you compare manuscripts? Did you investigate the canonicity of Shakspeare's various plays? Did you ransack the past to know the value of the latest theory that there never was a Will. Shakspeare save as a nom de plume for Lord Bacon? Did you inquire into the origin of his several plots, and study to know how much of his work was really his own and how much was borrowed from foreign sources. Or did you leave that all to the critics, and take the Shakspeare of today, and gather what instruction you might therefrom?"

Mr. Gear nodded his head slowly, and thoughtfully, as if he partially perceived the meaning of my answer. But he made no other response.

"There is much in common between us, Mr. Gear," I continued earnestly, "though much, very much that is not. We can find plenty of subject for fruitless debate no doubt. Can we find none for agreement and mutual helpfulness? Jesus of Nazareth you honor as first among men. You revere His noble life, His sublime death, His incomparable teachings. So do I. That noble life we can read together, Mr. Gear, and together we may emulate His example without a fruitless debate whether it be divine or no. Those incomparable teachings we can study together, that together we may catch the spirit that dictated them, without a theological controversy as to their authority. And even that sublime death I should hope we might contemplate together, without contention, though in the suffering Christ you see only a martyr, and I behold my Saviour and my God."

He made no answer, still stood silent. But he no longer looked at me with his sharp eyes. They had retired beneath his shaggy eyebrows as though he would search his own soul through and through, and read its verdict. He told me afterwards the story of his battle; I guessed it even then.

"We may not agree on the Gospel of John, Mr. Gear," said I, "but we shall not quarrel about the Golden Rule and the Sermon on the Mount."

"Mr. Laicus," said Mr. Gear at length, very slowly. "I thank you for coming to me. I thank you for speaking plainly and frankly as you have; I thank you for the respect which you have shown to my convictions. They are honest, and were not arrived at without a struggle and some self sacrifice. You are the first Christian," he added bitterly "that ever paid them the regard of a respectful hearing. I will join you in that Bible Class for this winter, and I will prove to you, infidel that I am, that I as well as a Christian, can respect convictions widely different from my own. If we quarrel it shall not be my fault."

"I believe you, Mr. Gear," said I. "God helping me it shall not be mine, and there's my hand upon it."

He grasped it warmly.

"When shall we begin?" said I.

"Next Sunday."

"Where?" said I.

"As you please?" said he.

"Here, or in my house, or at the church parlors, or wherever we can gather the young men," said I.

"The mill school-house is better than either," said he. "The boys will come there. They are used to it."

"The mill school-house be it," said I. "Next Sunday afternoon at 3 o'clock. I will bring the Bibles; you will bring the boys."

"As many as I can," said he.

"Jennie," said I that evening. "Mr. Gear and I are going to take the Bible Class together."

Tears stood in her eyes as she looked up at me with that smile I love so much. But she only said. "I knew you would succeed John."

CHAPTER X.
The Deacon's Second Service.

IT has been made the subject of some comment lately that Deacon Goodsole habitually absents himself from our Sabbath evening service. The pastor called the other day to confer with me on the subject; for he has somehow come to regard me as a convenient adviser, perhaps because I hold no office and take no very active part in the management of the Church, and so am quite free from what may be called its politics. He said he thought it quite unfortunate; not that the Deacon needed the second service himself, but that, by absenting himself from the house of God, he set a very bad example to the young people of the flock. "We cannot expect," said he, somewhat mournfully, "that the young people will come to Church, when the elders themselves stay away." At the same time he said he felt some delicacy about talking with the Deacon himself on the subject. "Of course," said he, "if he does not derive profit from my discourses I do not want to dragoon him into hearing them."

I readily promised to seek an occasion to talk with the Deacon, the more so because I really feel for our pastor. When I first came to Wheathedge he was full of enthusiasm. He has various plans for adding attractiveness and interest to our

Sabbath-evening service, which has always flagged. He tried a course of sermons to young men. He announced sermons on special topics. Occasionally a political discourse would draw a pretty full house, but generally it was quite evident that the second sermon was almost as much of a burden to the congregation as it was to the minister. Latterly he seems to have given up these attempts, and to follow the example of his brethren hereabout. He exchanges pretty often. Quite frequently we get an agent. Occasionally I fancy, the more from the pastor's manner than from my recollection, that he is preaching an old sermon. At other times we get a sort of expository lecture, the substance of which I find in my copy of Lange when I get home. Under this treatment the congregation, never very large, has dwindled away to quite diminutive proportions; and our poor pastor is quite discouraged. Until about six weeks ago Deacon Goodsole was always in his pew. I think his falling off was the last straw.

Last Sabbath evening, on my way to church, I stopped, according to promise, to see the Deacon. As I went up the steps I heard the sound of music, and waited a moment lest I should disturb the family's evening devotions. But as the music continued, and presently the tune changed, I concluded to knock. Nettie, the Deacon's youngest daughter, who by the way is a great favorite with me, answered the knock almost instantly. The open hymn-book was in her hand, and before I could get time to ask for the Deacon, she had, in her charmingly impulsive way, dragged me in, snatched my hat from my hand, deposited it on the table, and pushed me into the parlor. In fact, before I well knew what I was about, I found myself in the big arm-chair with Nettie in my lap, taking part in the Deacon's second service.

His family were all about him, including the stable boy, whose hair looked as sleek as the Deacon's horse. For the Deacon has some queer notions about the duties of employers to their servants, and, though the very kindest of men, is generally thought by the neighbors to be "a queer stick." The Deacon's wife, who has a very sweet soprano voice, which, however, she never could be persuaded to use in our choir, was presiding at the piano. The children all had their hymn and tune-books, and they were "singing round"--each member of the family selecting a hymn in turn. As they were limited to two verses each--except where two clubbed together to secure an entire hymn--the exercise was not prolonged, and certainly did not become tedious. After the singing, the Deacon asked the children if they were ready with their verses. They all raised their hands. The Deacon then repeated a short piece of poetry, his wife followed, and then all the children one after another, even down to Bob--a little three-year-old, who just managed to lisp out, with a charming mixture of pride and bashfulness,

> Jesus, tender Seperd,
> Has' thou died faw me,
> Make me vewy fwankful
> In my heart to thee.

Then the Deacon took down the family bible and opened it to the story of Joseph. He asked the children how far he had got. They answered him very sagely, and their responses to a few questions which he put to them showed that they understood what had gone before. Then he read part of one chapter, that which describes the beginning of the famine, and, asking Joe to bring him the full volume of Stanley's Jewish Church, he read the admirable description of an Egyptian famine which it contains. By this time Bob was fast asleep in his mother's arms. But all the rest of us kneeled down and repeated the Lord's prayer with the Deacon--another of his queer notions. The neighbors think he is inclined to be an Episcopalian, because he wants it introduced into the church service, but he says he does not really think that the Lord was an Episcopalian, and if he was it would not be any good reason for not using his prayer. Then the children kissed good-night, all round, and went to bed. Mrs. Goodsole took Bob off to his crib, and the Deacon and I were left alone. It was long past time for church service to begin, so I abandoned all idea of going to church, and opened to the Deacon at once the object of my errand. I told him very frankly that we not only missed him from the church, but that the pastor felt that his example was an unfortunate one, and that the church generally were afraid he was growing luke-warm in the Master's service, and I gently reminded him of the apostle's direction not to forget the assembling of ourselves together.

"Well," said he--though in trying to give his answer in his own language, I am obliged to condense the conversation of half-an-hour into a single paragraph--"Well, I will tell you how it is. You know I used to be pretty regular in attendance on church, and in fact a pretty busy man on Sundays. We had breakfast early. Right after breakfast I sat down to look over my Sunday-school lesson for the last time. At nine o'clock I went to Sunday-school, where I had a Bible-class. At half-past ten came church. After service I had barely time to get a lunch, and then had to hurry away to our Mission. We almost always had some sort of a teachers' meeting after the regular session, so that it was generally tea-time before I got home. After tea I was off to church again. I almost always woke up Monday morning tired, and a little cross. My children are pretty good ones, I think, but they had a queer distaste for Sunday, which I put down to total depravity. And, strangest of all, my wife, who only went to church Sunday morning, and would not even sing in the choir, seemed to be as tired Monday morning as I was, only as it was washing-day she could not sleep as late. About two months ago I was laid up with a boil, and could not go to church. Of course I did not have my Sunday-school lesson to learn, and I was surprised to notice, for the first time, how hard my wife had to work to get the children off to Sunday-school. They stayed at church--as they always do--and for an hour after dinner they got along very well, reading their library books, but then began the labors of the day. First I heard Joe out in the yard frolicking with the dog, and rousing all the neighborhood with his racket. Of course I called him in. Next I heard my wife calling Lucy and Nettie to come down out of the swing. The next thing Bob was playing horse with the chairs in the parlor. So it went all the afternoon. The children had nothing to do. They could not read Sunday-school books all day. I am heterodox enough to wonder how they can read them at all--and of course they got into all sorts of mischief. And when at last poor Bobby came to me in utter despair, and lisped out, "Papa, what did God make Sunday for?" I broke down. I gathered the children about me, and proposed to them this evening service. I told them that if they would learn a hymn every Sunday I would stay at home in the evening with them. They caught at the idea enthusiastically. There is no law about it. They need not learn if they do not want to. But even Bobby has caught the enthusiasm, and gets a book and goes to his mamma every Sunday afternoon to teach him a verse. I have given up my class in the Mission, and made one of my Sunday-school Bible-class take it. I lie down and take a little nap after dinner. Then I learn my own hymn, and make my preparation for our evening service. About an hour before tea the children gather about me in the arbor and I read to them. I have just got Dr. Newton's "Bible Wonders," and am reading it chapter by chapter.

My wife takes that opportunity to rest. The consequence is that we both really get refreshed, instead of jaded out by our Sunday, and I think the children really look forward with anticipations of delight to its coming. "My Bible," continued the Deacon good naturedly, "says something about resting on Sunday. I wish our pastor would tell us what that means sometime."

I told the Deacon I thought he ought to tell his brethren, at some prayer-meeting, the reason why he stayed away from church; that it was due both to himself and to them. He agreed to do so. As for myself I am somewhat puzzled. I do not want our pastor left to preach to empty pews. But I am greatly enamored of the Deacon's second service.

CHAPTER XI.
Our Pastor Resigns.

ALL Wheathedge is in a fever of excitement. "Blessings brighten as they take their flight." We have just learned that we have enjoyed for these several years the ministry of one of the most energetic, faithful, assiduous, eloquent, and devoted "sons of thunder," in the State. We never appreciated our dominie aright till now. But now no one can praise him too highly. The cause of this his sudden rise in public estimation is a very simple one. He has been called to a New York City parish. And he has accepted the call.

This is a curious world, and the most curious part of it is the Church. While he stayed we grumbled at him. Now he leaves we grumble because he is going.

I first heard of this matter a couple of weeks ago. No. Some rumors of what was threatened were in the air last summer. One Sabbath, in our congregation, were three gentlemen, in one of whom I recognised my friend, Mr. Eccles, of the--street Presbyterian Church of New York City. He was there again the second Sabbath. It was rumored then that he was on a tour of inspection. But I paid little attention to the rumor. In October, our pastor takes his vacation. I thought it a little strange that he should spend half of it in New York, and seek rest from preaching in his own pulpit by repeating his sermons in a metropolitan church. But I knew the state of his purse. I therefore gave very little heed to the gossip which my wife repeated to me, and which she had picked up in the open market. For Sunday is market day, and the church is the market for village gossip in Wheathedge. And Jennie, who is constitutionally averse to change, was afraid we were going to lose our pastor, and said as much. But I laughed at her fears.

However, the result proved that the gossips were, for once, right. About two weeks ago, Mr. and Mrs. Work came into my house in a high state of subdued excitement. Mr. Work handed me a letter. It was a call to the--street Presbyterian Church in New York--salary $4000 a year. It was accompanied by a glowing portraiture of the present and prospective usefulness which this field opened. The church was situated in a part of the city where there were few or no churches. The ward had a population of over fifty thousand, a large majority of whom attended no church. More than half were Protestants. There was a grand field for Sabbath-school labor. The church was thoroughly united. Its financial condition was satisfactory, and its prospects encouraging. And the hearts of the people had been led to unite as one man upon Mr. Work.

"I cannot but think," said Mr. Work, "that it is Providential. The position is entirely unsought. Yet I do not really feel equal to a place of such importance. I am sensible how much wider is the sphere of usefulness. But am I able to fill it? That is the question."

"Well, for my part," said Mrs. Work, "I confess that I am mercenary. There is a great deal of difference between $1,200 and $4,000 a year. It will put us at our ease at once. And just think what advantages for the children."

They wanted my advice. At least they said so. It is my private opinion that they wanted me to advise them to go. I told them I would think about it and tell them the result the next week. They agreed meanwhile to wait.

There were two considerations which operated on their minds, one usefulness, the other salary. I undertook to measure those two considerations.

The very next day gave me an opportunity to investigate the former. I met my friend Mr. Eccles at Delmonico's. We talked over the affairs of his church at the table.

"You are trying to get our minister away from us," said I.

"Yes," said he. "And I think we shall get him. He is a sound man--just the man to build us up."

"And how are you prospering?" said I.

"Capitally," said he. And then he proceeded, in answer to a cross-examination, to interpret his reply. The Church had almost a monopoly of the ward. Its debt was but $10,000, which was in a mortgage on the property. There was also a small floating debt which would be easily provided for. It paid its former pastor $4,000, just what it offered Mr. Work. Its pew rents were about $3,500. The deficiency was considerable, and had to be made up every year by subscription. "But our minister," said M. Eccles, confidentially, "was a dull preacher. I liked him--my wife liked him. All the church folks liked him. But he did not draw. And it is not enough in New York city, Mr. Laicus, for a minister to be a good man, or even a good preacher. He must draw. That's it; he must draw. I expect the first year, that we shall have a deficit to make up, but if next spring we don't let all our pews, why I am mistaken in my man, that's all. Besides they say he is a capital man to get money out of people, and we must pay off our debt or we will never succeed, and that's a fact."

I got some figures from Mr. Eccles, and put them down. They give the following result:

Income. 200 pews at present average-$30 a pew $6,000

Expenses. Salary $4,000 Interest 700 Music 1,200 Sexton, fuel, light, &c. 1,200 Total $7,100

When I showed the footing to Mr. Eccles he shrugged his shoulders. "We shall have to raise our pew rents," said he. "They are unconscionably low, and we must pay off our debt. Then we are all right. And if we get the right man, one that can draw, he will put our heads above water."

With that we separated.

Not, however, till I got some further information from him. He remarked casually that he had a notion of moving out of town, and asked me about prices at Wheathedge. "It costs a fortune to live here," said he. "My wife has an allowance of $300 a month for household and personal expenses. My clothing and extras cost me another $500. And the "sundries" are awful. You can't go out of your house for less than a dollar. I have no doubt my incidentals are another $500. It is awful--awful."

I advised him to move up to Wheathedge, the more cordially because I have a lot I would like to sell him for about a thousand dollars. I really believe he is thinking seriously of it.

The next day I went into the office of my friend Mr. Rental, the broker. I told him I was looking for a house for a friend, and asked the prices. He showed me a list-rents $2,000, $2,500, $3,000. They were too high. Would property in Brooklyn or Jersey City do? No. It must be in New York. It must be in the -- ward. It must be a good, comfortable, plain house, without any show or pretension.

"There are none such to let in the city," said Mr. Rental. "Land costs too much. The few plain houses are all occupied by their owners." The very best he could do was one house, half a mile from the church, for $1,800. He had one other for $1,500, but it was opposite an immense stable, and had neither cellar nor furnace, and croton only on the first floor. I thanked him and said I would look in again if either of them suited.

Last week, according to appointment, our pastor and his wife came in for a second consultation.

"There are," said I, "two considerations which might lead you to accept this call-increased usefulness and increased salary. I do not deny the importance of a New York city parish, nor fail to recognize the good work the city ministers are doing. But you must not fail to recognize the difficulties of the situation. New York is sensation-mad. The competition in churches is as great as in business. There are perhaps half a dozen men of genius who fill their churches with ease, or whose churches are filled because they are the resort of "good society." The rest of the ministers are compelled to devote three-quarters of their energies to keeping a congregation together, the other quarter to doing them good. They accomplish the first, sometimes by patient, persistent, assiduous, unwearying pastoral labor, sometimes by achieving a public reputation. sometimes by the doubtful expedient of sensational advertisements of paradoxical topics. But in whatever way they do it the hardest part of their work, a part, country parsons know next to nothing of, is to get and keep a congregation. What you are wanted for at the--street Presbyterian Church is to 'build it up.' The one quality for which you are commended is the capacity to 'draw.' Doubtless there are devout praying men and women who will measure your work by its spiritual results, by the conversion of sinners and the growth in grace of Christians. But what the financial managers want is one who will fill up their empty pews, enable them to add fifty per cent. to the rentals, and in some way pay off their debt. That will be their measure of your usefulness."

It was quite evident that my good pastor and his wife thought me uncharitable. Was I?

"As to salary," said I, "you country clergymen are greatly mistaken in supposing that city salaries are prizes to be coveted. Six thousand dollars is only a moderately fair support for a New York clergyman, and there are comparatively few who get it. You must pay at least $1,800 rent. You must dress as well as the average of your best families. You must neither be ashamed for yourselves nor for your children in the best society. You must keep open house. You must set a good table. You must be "given to hospitality." You must take a lead in organizing the missionary and charitable movements of your Church, which you cannot do without some money. You must be ready to co-operate in great public, church, and philanthropic movements. You must take a vacation of six weeks every summer, which of itself, at the lowest estimate, will cost you $150 or $200 a year. I have made some inquiries of three or four economical friends in New York. Here is the result of my inquiries. You may reduce the figures a little. But it will require quite as much economy to live in New York on $4,000 a year as in Wheathedge on $1,200."

With that I showed them the following memorandum:

Rent $1,800 Household expenses (a low estimate) 1,800 Dress for Mrs. Work and the two children 600 Dress and personal expenses of Mr. Work 500 Summer vacation 150 Incidentals 500

$5,350

Mr. and Mrs. Work thanked me for my advice, and took my memorandum home with them. But it was quite evident that Mrs. Work was not satisfied that $4,000 was not a great advance on $1,200. And I was not at all surprised when Mr. Work read his resignation from the pulpit last Sabbath. Next Sabbath he preaches his farewell sermon.

I hope I may prove a false prophet. But I think Mrs. Work will find her arithmetical powers taxed in New York as they never were in Wheathedge, and I shall be more pleased than I can tell if in five years Mr. Work does not retire from his post a disappointed man, or find that he has purchased success at the price of his health, if not his life.

Meanwhile we are beginning already to look about for his successor.

CHAPTER XII.
The Committee on Supply hold an informal Meeting.

MR. Work has preached his last sermon. A committee has been appointed to supply the pulpit, and secure a candidate for the pastorate. I believe this sort of business is generally left to the session; but on Deacon Goodsole's motion a special committee was appointed partly out of respect to the congregational element which is considerable in this church, and partly, I suspect, as a compliment to Mr. Wheaton. It consists of Mr. Wheaton and Mr. Gear, on behalf of the society, and Deacon Goodsole, Mr. Hardcap and myself on behalf of the church. I forgot to mention that since our Bible-class was commenced, Mr. Gear has begun to attend church, though not very regularly. Mr. Goodsole nominated Mr. Gear on the committee, and of course he was elected. I was rather sorry for I would have preferred that he did not know about the internal workings of this church. I do not think it will enhance his respect for religious institutions. Still I could make no objection. I did make objections to taking a place on the committee myself, but Jennie persuaded me to relinquish them. She has often heard me arguing that politics is a duty, that citizens are bound to take and administer public office for the benefit of the State. By a neat little turn she set all these arguments against me, and as I could not answer them I was obliged to yield. Our wives' memories are sometimes dreadfully inconvenient.

Our committee held a sort of informal meeting last night, at the Post-Office, where we all met by chance, the usual way. In the Post-Office is the news exchange of Wheathedge, where we are very apt to meet about the time of the arrival of the evening mail. Deacon Goodsole had been delegated to get a supply for the next two Sabbaths till we could discuss the merits of candidates. He reported that he had engaged the Rev. Mr. Elder, of Wheatensville. "He has the merest pittance of a salary," said the Deacon, "and I knew the twenty dollars would be acceptable to him. Besides which he is not only an excellent man but a sound preacher."

"Why wouldn't he be the man for us?" said I.

Mr. Wheaton exclaimed against me, "Too old," said he.

"Besides he's got five children," said Mr. Hardcap.

"What's that got to do with it?" said I. "So has Deacon Goodsole; but he's none the worse for that."

"We can't afford to support a man with a large family," said Mr. Hardcap. "We must get a young man. We can't possibly afford to pay over $1,200 a year, and we ought not to pay over $1,000."

"Oh!" said I; "do we grade the ministers' salaries by the number of the minister's children?"

"Well we have to consider that, of course," said Mr. Hardcap.

"Solomon wasn't so wise as he is generally thought to be," said Mr. Gear sarcastically, "or he never would have written that sentence about blessed is he whose quiver is full of them!"

"Well," said Mr. Hardcap, "all I've got to say is, if you get a man here with five children you can pay his salary, that's all."

"When you take a job Mr. Hardcap," said I, "do you expect to be paid according to the value of the work or according to the size of your family?"

"Oh! that's a very different thing," said Mr. Hardcap, "very different."

"Any way," said Mr. Wheaton, "Mr. Elder is entirely out of the question-- entirely so. Mr. Laicus can hardly have proposed him seriously."

"Why out of the question, gentlemen?" said I. "He is a good preacher. Our congregation know him. He is a faithful, devoted pastor. We shall do Wheatensville no injustice, for it cannot give him a support. As to age, he is certainly not infirm. I do not believe he is a year over forty-five."

"No! no!" said Mr. Wheaton, decidedly. "It is utterly out of the question. We must have a young man, one who is fresh, up with the spirit of the age; one who can draw in the young men. The Methodists are getting them all."

"And the young girls too," said Mr. Gear dryly.

I wish Mr. Gear were not on this committee. The Deacon meant well. But he made a blunder.

"Very well, then, gentlemen," said I; "if we want a fresh man let us go right to the theological seminary and get the best man we can find there."

"The seminary!" said Mr. Wheaton. He received this suggestion even more disdainfully than the previous one. "We must have a man of experience, Mr. Laicus. A theological student would never do."

"Experience without age!" said I; "that's a hard problem to solve. For the life of me I do not see how we are going to do it."

"Well you must consider, Mr. Laicus," said Mr. Wheaton, adding force to his words by a gentle and impressive gesture with his forefinger, "that this is a very important and a very peculiar field-a very peculiar field indeed, Mr. Laicus. And it requires a man of very peculiar qualifications. It is really a city field," he continued. "To all intents and purposes Wheathedge is a suburb of New York City. In the summer our congregation is very largely composed of city people. They are used to good preaching. They won't come to hear a commonplace preacher. And at the same time we have a very peculiar native population. And then, apart from our own people, there is the Mill village which really belongs to our parish, and which our pastor ought to cultivate. All these various elements combine to make up a diverse and conflicting population. And it will require a man of great energy, and great prudence, and no little knowledge of human nature, and practical skill in managing men, to get along here at all. I know more about Wheathedge than you do, Mr. Laicus, and I assure you that it is a very peculiar field."

I believe that in the estimation of supply committees all fields are very peculiar fields. But I did not say anything.

"And we need a very peculiar man?" said Mr. Gear inquiringly.

"Yes," said Mr. Wheaton, decidedly; "a man of peculiar abilities and qualifications."

"Well then," said Mr. Gear, "I hope you are prepared to pay a peculiar salary. I don't know much about church matters gentlemen. I don't know what you put me on the committee for. But in my shop if I want a peculiar man I have to pay a peculiar salary."

There was a little laugh at this sally, but Mr. Gear evidently meant no joke, and as evidently Mr. Wheaton did not take any.

"Well," said I, "so far as salary goes I am prepared to vote for an increase to $1,500 and a parsonage. I don't live on less than twice that."

Mr. Hardcap struck his hands down resolutely into his pockets and groaned audibly.

"I am afraid we can't get it, Mr. Laicus," said Mr. Wheaton. "I believe a minister ought to have it, but I don't see where its coming from. We musn't burden the parish."

"And I believe," I retorted, "that the laborer is worthy of his hire; and we must not burden the pastor."

"For my part," said Mr. Hardcap, "I won't give my consent to a dollar over $1,200 a year. I ain't goin' to encourage ministerial luxury nohow."

"Well, for my part," said Mr. Wheaton, "I don't care so much about that. But we must have a first rate man. He has to preach here in the summer time to city congregations. They are critical sir, critical. And we have got to have just as good a man as the Broadway Tabernacle. But as to paying a city salary, that you know is absurd, Mr. Laicus. We can't be expected to do that."

"Bricks without straw," murmured Mr. Gear.

Just then the Post-Office window opened, and we made a rush for our mail. But before we separated we agreed to hold a formal meeting at my house a week from the following Thursday evening for a further canvass of the whole matter.

Meanwhile I am perplexed by the double problem that our informal meeting has suggested. I have been sitting for half an hour pondering it. The children have long since gone to bed. I have finished my evening paper, and written my evening letters. The fire has burned low, and been replenished. Jennie sits by my side engaged in that modern imitation of Penelope's task, the darning of stockings. And for half an hour, only the ticking of the clock and the sighing of the wind outside have disturbed the silence of the room.

"Jennie," said I, at length, "when I told you to-night of our talk at the Post-Office you said you hoped we would get a young man. Why?"

"Why?" said Jennie.

"Yes," said I. "I can understand why Mr. Hardcap wants a young man. It is for the same reason that he employs half taught apprentices in his shop. They are cheap. Of course our good friend Maurice Mapleson, with neither wife nor children, can more easily lay up money on $1,000 a year than Mr. Elder, with his five children can on $1,500 or $2,000. But I don't think you and I, Jennie, want to economize on our minister."

"I am sure we don't John," said Jennie.

"And I can understand why Mr. Wheaton wants a young minister. Young ministers do draw better, at least at first. There is a certain freshness and attractiveness in youth. Curiosity is set agog in watching the young minister, and still more in watching his young bride. A ministerial honey-moon is a godsend to a parish. Whether we ought to hire our pastors to set curiosity agog and serve the parish as a nine-day's wonder may be a question. But I suspect that we very often do. But, Jennie, I hope you and I don't want a minister to serve us as food for gossip."

"I am sure not, John,' said Jennie earnestly.

"Why is it then, Jennie," said I, "that you and I want youth in our minister? Young lawyers and young doctors are not in requisition. Age generally brings confidence even when it does not endow with wisdom. I believe that Judge Ball's principal qualification for his office was his bald head and grey beard. When you discovered a couple of grey hairs on my head a little while ago, I was delighted. I should like to multiply them. Every grey hair is worth a dollar. Dr. Curall has hard work to get on in his profession because he is so young and looks still younger than he is. If there was such a thing as grey dye it would pay him to employ it. Lawyers and doctors must be old-ministers must be young. Why, Jennie?"

"Perhaps," said Jennie, "we want in our ministers enthusiasm more than wisdom."

"Enthusiasm," said I. "That might do for the Methodists. But it does not apply to the Congregationalists, and the Episcopalians, and the staid and sober Presbyterians."

"I don't know about that," said Jennie. "What we want of our preachers is not so much instruction as inspiration. We want some body not to think for us but to set us to thinking. Our souls get sluggish, and they want to be stirred up. I do not want some one to prove the authority of the ten commandments, John, but some one to make me more earnest to obey them. I do not care much about Dr. Argure's learned expositions of the doctrine of atonement. But I do want some one who shall make me realize more and more that Jesus died for me."

"And what has that to do with youth, Jennie?" said I.

"I don't know," said Jennie, thoughtfully; "unless it is that the truth seems somehow new and fresh to the young minister. Besides it is not youth, John, altogether. It is freshness, and warmth, and enthusiasm, and spiritual life. Mr. Beecher is not young nor is Spurgeon, nor Dr. Hall, nor Dr. Tyng, nor John B. Gough. But they are all popular. Father Hyatt isn't young, John, but I had rather hear him than

Dr. Argure any day."

I rather think Jennie is right. It is not youth we want at Wheathedge, but spiritual life and earnestness. At least it is to be thought of.

But as to salary-how we are to get a first class man at a third class salary puzzles me. I shall have to refer that to Mr. Wheaton. He is the financier of our church I believe.

CHAPTER XIII.
Maurice Mapleson declines to submit to a competitive examination.

"I have a letter from Maurice Mapleson," said I to Jennie.

"What does he say? Will he come?" said she eagerly.

"No!" said I. "He won't come."

"I am sorry," said she. "It's too bad of him."

"You won't think so, my dear," said I, "when you hear his letter. You'll be more sorry; but you'll think better of him than you did before."

We were at the tea-table. It is the rule of our meal hour to have the conversation one in which the children can engage-in which at all events they can take an interest. So the topic was suffered to drop till they were in bed, and we were alone in the library.

Maurice Mapleson was a young minister that I thought a good deal of. So when two Sundays before, Mr. Wheaton suggested him to me as a successor to our retiring pastor, I welcomed the suggestion.

"You know that young Mapleson, don't you Mr. Laicus," said he, "who preached for us two Sundays last summer. I think he stopped at your house."

I assented.

"I wish you would write him, quite informally you know, to come down and preach for us a Sunday or two. The folks at our house were quite taken with him, and I think the people were generally. I shouldn't wonder if he were the 'coming man,' Mr. Laicus."

So that evening I stayed at home from church and wrote to him. I remembered what Mr. Wheaton had said about this being a peculiar parish, and our people a peculiar people, and I waxed eloquent as I wrote. I reminded Mr. Mapleson of our glorious scenery. I told him we were but a suburb of New York and he would have a city congregation, and I did not tell him that he would have to pay very nearly city prices for everything, and would not have anything that would approximate a city salary. I told him of the Mill village and the opportunities of Christian labor it opened before him. I assured him that he would find the people remembering him kindly, and ready to welcome him warmly. In short I considered myself retained as advocate In re the Calvary Presbyterian Church, and I rather laid myself out to produce an impression.

And I rather flatter myself that I did produce an impression. But I did not get a verdict. Here is his answer as I read it to Jennie that evening. KONIWASSET COR-NERS, Tuesday. JOHN LAICUS, ESQ.,

Dear Sir,--I thank you very warmly for your kind letter of the 6th instant. Kind it certainly is, and though I must decline the invitation it presents so cordially to me, I am none the less grateful for it, notwithstanding the fact that it has been a strong and not easily resisted temptation to violate my settled convictions of duty.

If I were writing formally to the committee it would be enough to decline your invitation without entering into any explanation. But the remembrance of the pleasant week I spent at your house last summer, and the tone of your letter, makes me feel as though I were writing to a personal friend. This is my excuse (if one is needed) for giving you more fully than I otherwise should, my reasons for declining. Those reasons are not in any way connected with the parish at Wheatedge. I am not insensible to the attractions which the place possesses as a residence, nor to that which the parish possesses as a field of labor. But I resolved when I first entered the ministry that I would never preach as a candidate. I never have, and I never will. I began my work in a mission school in New York City, while I was yet in the Seminary. When I left the Seminary, Mr. Marcus who is one of the trustees of the mission asked me to come up to this church. It is a sort of mission among the miners, being half supported by Mr. Marcus who is one of the directors of the Koniwasset Coal Co. I came for six months. The congregation asked me to remain, and I remained. And here I purpose to remain till God shall call me to another field.

Another field I will not seek, though I should live and die here. I pretend to believe that Christ is my Bishop; and I shall not move without orders from him.

So long as I am pastor here I cannot preach with honor as a candidate in other parishes. I know other ministers do it-and I do not judge them. But I cannot. Suppose my people were to take advantage of my absence for a week to try a candidate. I wonder what I should say to that. And I cannot see that settled ministers have any more right to try other parishes with reference to a change of place, than parishes with settled ministers have to try other ministers with reference to a change of pastors. In a word I do not believe in free-love as applied to churches.

But apart from that I cannot preach as a candidate. The minister is ordained to preach to convert impenitent sinners and to build up and strengthen Christians. Do you suppose I should do either if I came to Wheathedge on your invitation to preach as a candidate? Not at all. The people would come to criticise, and I should go to be criticised. They would be judges and would expect to put me through my ministerial faces to try me. Come, the congregation says in effect to me in such an invitation, let us see how you can preach, exhibit your proficiency in the doctrines, try your skill in arousing sinners, see what you can do in interesting the saints, read us a hymn or two, as a test of your elocution, and display to us your "gifts in prayer;" and then when the service is over, spend a week and take tea with two or three of our principal families and show us what your social qualifications are, and give our children an opportunity to quiz you. That it is in effect Mr. Laicus, though it may seem somewhat presumptuous in me to say it. And to such a quizzing I am not at all inclined to submit. I never preached but one trial sermon-that was when I was licensed and I never mean to preach another.

Imagine Paul preaching as a candidate to the people of Athens or Corinth, and submitting his claims as an apostle to the popular verdict!

Or imagine, Mr. Laicus, a client coming to you and saying I have an important case to be tried sir, and I think of placing it in your hands. Will you oblige me by making a neat little speech for me. I want to see what kind of a speech you can make.

Since I wrote that last sentence I have read this letter over, and have been on the point, two or three times, of tearing it up and sending in its place a simple declination. But I feel as though I were writing to a friend, and it shall go. I am sorry it must be so. I should like to go to Wheathedge. That it is a beautiful place, and has pleasant people, and is a far more important field of labor than this I recognize fully; and then, what possibly influences me quite as much, Helen, whom your wife knows very well, is waiting patiently for me, and I am waiting impatiently for her, and I never can marry on the little pittance I receive here. But she is of one mind with me in this matter, I know, for we have often talked it over together, and she holds me nobly to my resolution. She, I am sure, would not have me write other than I do.

My kind regards to Mrs. Laicus and my sincere thanks to yourself. A kiss to Harry too, if you please, if he is not too old to take one. The baby I have never seen. Yours sincerely, MAURICE MAPLESON.

"Well," said Jennie after I had finished reading the letter, "I believe he is right; but I am sorry John; sorrier than I was before."

"Sorry that he won't come, Jennie?"

"Sorry that he is right," said Jennie. "That is, if he is right."

"Do you doubt it, Jennie?" said I.

"Well I don't know, John. I go with him. I like him better for his letter. I cannot gainsay it. And yet it seems to me that it puts the ministers in a rather hard position."

"Yes?" said I interrogatively.

"Yes," said Jennie. "You know perfectly well John that our church here wouldn't call a man that isn't settled somewhere. The very fact that he was out of a parish,, would be almost conclusive against him. And they won't call a man without trying him. Must Maurice Mapleson live and die in that little out of the way corner? And if he is ever going to get out of it, how is it to come about? How does a minister have any chance for a change if he takes such a ground as that? It's high and noble John, and I honor him for it; but I am afraid it isn't practicable."

"Little woman," said I, "whatever is truly high and noble is practicable, and you would be the first to tell me so another time. Don't let our wanting Maurice Mapleson here blind us to that."

Jennie smiled her assent. "Well John," said she, "what you are going to do about it?"

"Do?" said I. "Nothing. There is nothing to be done, except to read Mr. Mapleson's letter to the committee, to-morrow night at our first meeting. And I am curious to see what they'll say to it."

CHAPTER XIV.
The Supply Committee hold
their first formal Meeting.

PLACE: James Wheaton's library.--Hour: seven and a half o'clock in the evening.--Present: James Wheaton, Thomas Gear, James Goodsole, Solomon Hardcap, and John Laicus.--John Laicus in the chair.

Laicus.:

--Gentlemen the first business in order is to appoint a secretary.

Deacon Goodsole.:

--Oh, you can keep the minutes. We don't want much of a record.

Laicus.:

--Very good, if that is agreed to. My minutes will be very simple.

James Wheaton.:

--That's all right. What do you hear from Mr. Mapleson? Anything?

Laicus.:

--Yes I have his letter in my pocket.

James Wheaton.:

--When will he come?

Laicus.:

--He declines to come.

James Wheaton,: [(astonished).]

--Declines to come. Why a church mouse would starve on the pittance they pay him at Koniwasset Corners. What's his reason?

Laicus.:

--His letter is a rather singular and striking one, gentlemen. Perhaps I had better read it.

Which he thereupon proceeds to do, slowly and distinctly, till he reaches the closing paragraphs, which he omits as being of a purely personal character.

James Wheaton.:

--That fellow's got stuff in him and no mistake. By Jove I believe if I was running this church I would take him on trust.

Solomon Hardcap.:

--I think it a very presumptuous letter. The idea. What does he expect? Does he think we're goin' to take a preacher without ever havin' heard him preach?

Deacon Goodsole.:

--We have heard him preach, Mr. Hardcap. He preached here two Sundays last summer. Don't you recollect?

Solomon Hardcap.:

--Yes. I remember. But I didn't take no notice of his sermons; he wan't preachin' as a candidate.

Mr. Gear.:

--Gentlemen I am not very much acquainted with church affairs and I don't think I understand this business very well. What do you mean by preaching as a candidate? I thought a candidate was a man who applied for an office. Am I to understand that whenever a pulpit is vacant the church expects different ministers to apply for it, and puts them on trial, and picks out the one it likes the best?

Mr. Hardcap.:

--That's it exactly.

Mr. Gear.:

--You don't really mean to say that any decent ministers apply for the place on those terms.

Deacon Goodsole,: [(warmly).]

--Indeed they do Mr. Gear. There is never any lack of candidates for a favorable parish. I have got half a dozen letters in my pocket now. One man writes and sends me copies of two or three letters of recommendation. Another gives me a glowing account of the revival that has followed his labors in other fields. Then there's a letter from a daughter that really moved me a good deal. She pleads hard for her father who is poor and is getting old, and needs the salary sadly-poor man.

Mr. Gear.:

--Well, all I have got to say, is that when any of those candidates come to preach I hope you'll notify me, and I'll stay away.

Mr. Hardcap.:

--I have no patience with these new fangled notions of these young up-start preachers. I reckon the ways our fathers got their preachers are good enough for us.

Mr. Gear.:

--And what do you say as to that point he makes about Paul's preaching as a candidate, Mr. Hardcap?

Mr. Hardcap.:

--Oh! that's different, altogether-very different. The apostle was inspired, Mr. Gear.

I notice that this is a very popular style of argument with Mr. Hardcap. Whenever he is posed in argument his never failing rejoinder is "Oh! that's different, altogether different." And I think I have observed that the Hardcap logic is not confined to Mr. Hardcap, but is in high regard in other quarters, where I should least look for it.

Mr. Gear.:

--Well I don't think much of apostolic authority myself. But I supposed the rest of you thought you were bound by any precedents Paul had set.

Mr. Hardcap.:

--It's mighty high seems to me for a young man to be making of himself out as good as the apostle Paul.

Mr. Wheaton.:

--I like that young Mapleson, and I like his letter. I wish we could get him. Is there any chance of persuading him to come, Mr. Laicus? not as a candidate you know, but just to preach, in good faith like any other man.

Mr. Gear shrugs his shoulders.

Laicus,: [(decidedly).]

--No! and I should not want to be the one to try.

Mr. Wheaton.:

--Well then who stands next on our list?

Mr. Gear.:

--Excuse me gentlemen, but if he can't come to us why shouldn't we go to him.

Why not try him as we would try any other man.

Deacon Goodsole.:

--How do you mean Mr. Gear?

Mr. Gear.:

--If I want a workman at my factory I don't invite one to come from my neighbor and try his hand for a day while I stand over and watch him. We try our apprentices that way, but never a good workman. I go to his shop, inquire as to his character, and examine the work that he has done. If he has done good work in another man's shop he will do it well in mine. At least that's the way we reason in our factory.

Mr. Hardcap.:

--That's a very different case Mr. Gear, altogether different.

Mr. Gear.:

--Suppose this Mr. Whats-his-name comes, what more will you know about him than you know now?

Deacon Goodsole.:

--We shall hear him preach and can judge for ourselves.

Mr. Gear.:

--One good sermon does not make a good preacher.

Mr. Wheaton.:

--No! But you don't need to drive a horse more than five miles to know what are his paces.

Mr. Gear.:

--I don't know much about church management but I like the tone of that man's letter, and I should like to know more about him. I believe if we were to appoint a committee to go out to Koniwasset Corners, hear him preach, look in on his Sabbath-school, find out what kind of a pastor he is, and in a word see what sort of work he's doing where he is now, we would get his measure a great deal better than we should get it by having him come here, and give us one of his crack sermons-even if he would do it, I honor him because he won't.

Deacon Goodsole.:

--I am afraid it wouldn't do Mr. Gear-not with our people. I wouldn't mind it myself.

Mr. Wheaton,: [(blandly).]

--You see Mr. Gear you don't understand church matters altogether. It would not be ecclesiastical-not at all.

Mr. Gear,: [(sarcastically and sotto voce).]

--I hope I may never learn.

Laicus,: [(desiring to prevent controversy).]

--Gentlemen, I for one agree with Mr. Gear. But we are evidently in the minority; so there is nothing more to be said about it. We both believe in government by the majority, and shall submit. What next, Deacon? Are there any of your letters you want to read to us?

Deacon Goodsole.:

--Oh no! It isn't worth while to read any of them. Though I am sorry for that poor old man and his pleading daughter.

Mr. Wheaton.:

--The Deacon's list are all too anxious.

Deacon Goodsole.:

--I suppose there is nothing to do but to pursue the usual course. I move that Mr. Laicus and Mr. Wheaton be appointed to open a correspondence with candidates.

Laicus,: [(decidedly).]

You must excuse me gentlemen. I don't believe in candidating, and I can't be accessory to it. I will substitute Deacon Goodsole's name for my own. And as so amended will put the motion.

As so amended the motion was put, and carried, and the committee on supply adjourned to meet at the call of Deacon Goodsole and Mr. Wheaton. But as we walked along toward my home, M. Gear remarked to me that he wished I would let him know when we got a parson so that he could come to church again; for said he, "I have no inclination to serve as a parson tester." And I confess I am quite of mind with him.

CHAPTER XV.
Our Christmas at Wheathedge.

IS there any reason why Episcopalians, Lutherans and Roman Catholics should have a monopoly of Christmas? Is its glorious old patron Saint partial? Has the Christ-child no gifts for us as well as for other folk? Have the December heavens no brightness-the angel host no song for "blue Presbyterians?" May we not come to the sacred manger too? Are our Church festivals so many that we need dread to add another? Is our religion so inclined to gayety and money-making that we need curb its joyous tendencies? The very air of Christmas is marvellous. The heavens are never so blue, the sun never shines with a profuser generosity. The very earth clothes itself in the spotless white of the heavenly robe, as if to prepare for the coming of its Lord.

Alas for him who does not believe in Christmas! May the ghost of Scrooge haunt him into a better mind.

This was what I mentally ejaculated to myself last Saturday afternoon after Mr. Hardcap's protest against our Christmas celebration.

The Sabbath morning previous, Miss Moore came to me mysteriously after church. "I want to walk home with you, Mr. Laicus," said she. I have a wife and children, and I felt safe. "I shall be delighted with the honor," I replied. But Miss Moore's honors are never empty ones. I knew that she wanted something; I wondered what. I had not long to wonder; for we had not crossed the road before she opened the subject.

"We are going to trim the Church for Christmas," said she, "and we want you to superintend getting the evergreens."

"What?" said I, aghast.

Confidentially, please not mention it, I have been in the habit for a good many years of taking my wife and my prayer-book to the Episcopal Church on Christmas-day. Dickens converted me to its observance ten years or more ago. But none are so sound as those who are tinged with heresy. And am I not a "blue Presbyterian?" It would not do to lend my countenance too readily to indecorous invasions of the sanctuary with festivals borrowed from the Roman Catholics. Besides, what would the elders say? I asked Miss Moore as much.

"Deacon Goodsole will lend us his pung," was the reply.

"And the trustees?" said I.

But Miss Moore never leaves a point unguarded.

"Young Wheaton is home from school," said she, "and he will go with you to the woods. He will call to-morrow, right after breakfast."

For a difficult piece of generalship give me a woman. Not fitted for politics! Why, they are born to it. Here was Miss Moore bent on trimming the church. And lawyer Laicus was to go in Deacon Goodsole's sleigh with the son of the President of the Board of Trustees to get the "trimmings." He who dares to complain after that enlists two dignitaries and one very respectable layman against him at the outset.

"Very well," said I, "I will go."

"Go!" said Miss Moore, "of course you'll go. Nobody doubted that. But I want to tell you where to go and what to get."

The next morning I was just finishing my second cup of coffee when I heard the jingle of bells, and, looking up, saw Jim Wheaton and the Deacon's sleek horse at my door. So, bidding Harry, who was to go too, "be quick," an exhortation that needed no repeating, we were very soon in the pung, armed I with a hatchet, Harry with a pruning knife.

That ride was one to be remembered. The air was crisp and clear. Just snow enough had fallen in the night to cover every black and noisome thing, as though all nature's sins were washed away by her Sabbath repentance, and she had commenced her life afresh. There was luxury in every inhalation of the pure air. The horse, more impatient than we, could scarcely wait for leave to go, and needed no word thereafter to quicken his flying feet. Down the hill, with merry ringing bells, ever and anon showered with flying snow from the horse's hoof; through the village street with a nod of recognition to Deacon Goodsole, who stood at his door to wave us a cheery recognition; round the corner with a whirl that threatens to deposit us in the soft snow and leave the horse with an empty sleigh; across the bridge, which spans the creek; up, with unabated speed, the little hill on the other side; across the railroad track, with real commiseration for the travelers who are trotting up and down the platform waiting for the train, and must exchange the joyous freedom of this day for the treadmill of the city, this air for that smoke and gas, this clean pure mantle of snow for that fresh accumulation of sooty sloshy filth; pass the school-house, where the gathering scholars stand, snowballs in hand, to see us run merrily by, one urchin, more mischievous than the rest, sending a ball whizzing after us; up, up, up the mountain road, for half a mile, past farm-houses whose curling smoke tell of great blazing fires within; past ricks of hay all robed in white, and one ghost of a last summer's scare-crow watching still, though the corn is long since in-gathered and the crows have long since flown to warmer climes; turning off, at last, from the highway into Squire Wheaton's wood road, where, since the last fall of snow, nothing has been before us, save a solitary rabbit whose track our dog Jip follows excitedly, till he is quite out of sight or even call.

Here we are at last. And here the evergeens are about us in a profusion which would make the eyes water of my honest friend the Dutch grocer who supplied me with my family trees so many years in New York. Our smoking nag is over his impatience now, and, being well blanketed, understands what is wanted of him quite as well as if he were tied, and stands as still as if he were Squire Slowgoes' fat and lazy "family horse." With pants tied snugly over our topboots to keep out the intruding snow, we plunge into the woods. The ringing blows of our hatchets on the cedar-trees bring down a mimic shower on our heads and backs. Young Wheaton understands his business, and shows me how the fairest evergreens are hid beneath the snow, and what rare forms of crystalline beauty conceal themselves altogether beneath this white counterpane. So, sometimes cutting from above and sometimes grubbing from below, we work an hour or more, till our pung is filled to its brim. Long before we have finished Jip has returned from his useless search, and the neighing horse indicates his impatience to be off again.

When we got back to the Church we found it warm with a blazing fire in the great stove, and bright with a bevy of laughing girls, who emptied our sleigh of its contents almost before we were aware what had happened, and were impatiently demanding more. Miss Moore had proposed just to trim the pulpit-oh! but she is a shrewd manager-and we had brought evergreens enough to make two or three. But the plans had grown faster by far than we could work. One young lady had remarked how beautiful the chandelier would look with an evergreen wreath; a second had pointed out that there ought to be large festoons draping the windows;

a third, the soprano, had declared that the choir had as good a right to trimming as the pulpit; a fourth, a graduate of Mount Holyoke, had proposed some mottoes, and had agreed to cut the letters, and Mr. Leacock, the store keeper, had been foraged on for pasteboard, and an extemporized table contrived on which to cut and trim them. So off we were driven again, with barely time to thaw out our half-frozen toes; and, in short, my half morning's job lengthened out to a long days hard but joyous work, before the pile of evergreens in the hall was large enough to supply the energies of the Christmas workers.

Of course, we must trim the Sunday school-room as well as the Church, for the children must have their Christmas; and trimmed it was, so luxuriantly that it seemed as though the woods had laid siege to and taken possession of the sanctuary, and that nature was preparing to join on this glad day her voice with that of man in singing praise to Him who brings life to a winter-wrapped earth, and whose fittest symbol, therefore, is the tree whose greenness not even the frosts of the coldest winter have power to diminish.

Of course Christmas itself passed without recognition. I went, as is my wont, with my wife and my prayer-book, to the Episcopal Church. Our Christmas waited till Sunday. A glorious day it was. The sun never shone more brightly. The crisp keenness was gone from the air. The balmy breath of spring was in it. The Church never was so full before and never has been since. The story of its decorations had been spread far and wide, and all Wheathedge flocked to see what the Presbyterians would make of Christmas. The pulpit, the walls, the gallery, the chandelier were festooned with wreaths of living green. A cross-O tempora! O mores!-of cedar and immortelles, stood on the communion table. Over the pulpit were those sublime words of the sublimest of all books, "He shall save His people from their sins." Opposite it, emblazoned on the gallery, was heaven and earth's fitting response to this sublime revelation, "Glory be to God on high." Miss Moore was better than her word. She managed both choir and minister. Both were in the spirit of the occasion. The parson never preached a better sermon than his Christmas meditation. The choir never sung a more joyous song of praise than their Christmas anthem. And before the influence of that morning's service I think the last objection to observing Christmas faded out.

For there had been some objections. I heard of two.

One came from Mr. Wheaton. Monday afternoon, going by the Church, he saw the door open, went in, found it full of busy workers; ceiling, aisles, pulpit, and gallery, strewed with evergreens, and the clatter of merry voices keeping pace with the busy fingers. It was his first intimation of what was going on.

"Heyday!" said he. "What is all this? Who authorized it, I should like to know?"

The chatter of merry voices ceased. The young ladies were in awe. Miss Moore was not there to answer for them. No one dared act as spoksman. Young Jim Wheaton was on a step-ladder rather dangerously resting on the backs of two pews. He was tacking the letter G to the gallery. He noticed the silence and discerned the cause.

"Father," said he, "I wish you would hold this ladder for me a minute. It is rather ticklish."

"Ah, Jim, is that you?" said the old man. Pride in Jim is the father's weak point. The ladder was held. Then his advice was asked about the placing of the mottoes; and it was given, and that was the last of Mr. Wheaton's objection.

The other objection came from Mr. Hardcap, the carpenter. I met him at the door of the church Saturday afternoon, just as the last rubbish had been swept out and we were closing the door.

"Looks beautiful, doesn't it Mr. Hardcap?" said I.

"They'd better have spent their time on their knees than with these fixins," growled Mr. Hardcap; "'twould ha' done the Church more good, a deal sight."

"Did you spend your time on your knees?" I could not refrain from asking.

But Mr. Hardcap did not answer.

CHAPTER XVI.
Mr. Gear Again.

OUR Bible class at the Mill has prospered greatly. Mr. Gear was better than his word. The first Sabbath he brought in over a dozen of his young men; the half dozen who were already in the Sabbath School joined us of course. Others have followed. Some of the children of the Mill village gathered curiously about the school-house door from Sunday to Sunday. It occurred to me that we might do something with them. I proposed it to Mr. Gear. He assented. So we invited them in, got a few discarded singing books from the Wheathedge Sabbath-school, and used music as an invitation to more. Mrs. Gear has come in to teach them. There are not over a dozen or twenty all told as yet. If the skating or the sliding is good they are reduced to five or six. Still the number is gradually increasing, and there are enough to constitute the germ of a possible Mission-school. I wish we had a Pastor. He might make something out of it.

Mr. Gear adheres to his pledge, and I to mine. We have no theological discussions in the class. Occasionally, indeed pretty frequently, we get on themes on which we are not agreed. But we never debate. Mr. Gear has made several attempts at a theological discussion out of the class, but I have avoided them. I hope he does not think I am afraid of discussion.

I am not. But I am convinced that no mere intellectual opinion is a sin. If Mr. Gear is in darkness it is because he neglects some known if not some recognized duty. My work is not to convince him of the error of his opinions. I probably never could do that. And his opinions are not of much consequence. My work is to find out what known duty he is neglecting, and press it home upon his conscience. And so far I have not discovered what it is. He is one of the most conscientious men I ever knew. Yet something is wanting in Mr. Gear. I believe he half thinks so himself. He is mentally restless and uneasy. He seems to doubt his own doubts, and to want discussion that he may strengthen himself in his own unbelief. But still I make no progress. Since that first night I have got no farther into his heart.

"John," said Jennie, "I wish you would call and see Mr. Gear. He has not been in church for six or eight weeks."

"It is no use," said I, "I have asked him once or twice, and he always says that he is not coming till we get a Pastor. He says he does not care to hear candidates; he does not consider himself a good judge of the article. 'Hardcap,' says he is a ministerial expert, but I am not."

"How is he getting on?" said Jennie.

"To tell the truth, Jennie, I don't know," I replied. "I don't see that he gets on at all. He seems to be just where he was."

Jennie drew a long sigh.

"Patience, Jennie, patience," said I, "time works wonders."

"No, John," said Jennie, "time never works. It eats, and undermines, and rots, and rusts, and destroys. But it never works. It only gives us an opportunity to work."

Perhaps Jennie is right. Perhaps we expect time to work for us, when time is only given us that we may work.

"Besides," said Jennie, "there is that volume of Theodore Parker's sermons which you borrowed of him the other day, you have never returned it."

No! And I had never read it. Our theme in Bible class had touched on prayer. After the class Mr. Gear had tried to get me into a theological discussion about prayer. I had been silent as to my own views, but had asked him for his. And he had handed me this volume in reply. It contained a sermon by Theodore Parker on the subject which Mr. Gear said expressed his own views exactly. Jennie's remark brought this volume to mind, I took it down from the shelf, opened to the sermon, and read it aloud to Jennie.

We both agreed that it was a good sermon, or rather, to speak more accurately, a sermon in which there was good. It is true that in it Mr. Parker inveighed against the orthodox philosophy of prayer; he denied that God could really be influenced or his plans changed. But on the duty of prayer he vehemently insisted. Mere philanthropy and humanity, he said, are not religion. There must also be piety. The soul must live in the divine presence; must inhale the Spirit of God; must utter its contrition, its weaknesses, its wants, and its thanks-givings to its Heavenly Father.

That evening's reading suggested a thought to me. The next evening I started for Mr. Gear's to try if it were time, and to try the practicability of the plan it had developed in my mind. Mr. Gear welcomed me cordially. Mrs. Gear went off almost immediately on pretence of putting the children to bed, and left us two alone together. I opened the conversation by handing her husband the volume of sermons and thanking him for it.

"What do you think of the sermon?" said he.

"I liked a great deal of it very much indeed," said I. "I believe you told me that you liked it."

"Very much," said he. "I think its one of Theodore Parker's ablest sermons."

"And you believe in it?" said I interrogatively.

"With all my heart," said he. "Who can believe that the Great Infinite First

Cause can be influenced, and his plans changed by the teasing of every one of his insignificant little creatures?"

"But the rest of the sermon," said I. "Do you believe that?"

Last Sunday Professor Strait preached for us. He preached against what he called humanitarianism. He said it was living without God; that there was very little difference between ignoring God and denying his existence, and that the humanitarians practically ignored him; that they believe only in men.

"It is not true," said Mr. Gear, somewhat bitterly. "You can see for yourself that it is not true. Theodore Parker believes in prayer as much as Professor Strait. I don't believe but that he prayed as much."

"And you agree with him?" said I, with a little affectation of surprise.

"Agree with him, Mr. Laicus!" said he, "of course I do. There can be no true religion without prayer, without piety, without gratitude to God, without faith in Him. Your Church has not the monopoly of faith in God, by any means, that it assumes to have."

"And you really believe in prayer?" said I.

"Believe in prayer? Why, of course I do. Do you take me for a heathen?" replied he, with some irritation.

"And every night," said I, "you kneel down and commend yourself to our Heavenly Father's protection? and every morning you thank him for His watchfulness, and beseech divine strength from Him to meet the temptations of the day; and every day you gather your family about His throne, that you may teach your children to love and reverence the Father you delight to worship?"

There was a long pause. Mr. Gear was evidently taken by surprise. He made no answer; I pressed my advantage.

"How is it, my friend?" said I.

"Well, n--no!" said he, "I can't honestly say that I do."

"You believe in prayer, and yet never pray," said I, "is that it?"

"It is so much a matter of mere habit, Mr. Laicus," said he, excusingly; "and I never was trained to pray."

"All your lifelong," said I, taking no heed of the excuse, "you have been receiving the goodness of God, and you never have had the courtesy to say so much as 'thank you.' All your lifelong you have been trespassing against Him, and never have begged his pardon, never asked his forgiveness. Is it so?"

There was a moment's pause. Then he turned on me almost fiercely.

"How can I thank him Mr. Laicus," said he "when you say that I do not love him, and cannot love him."

"Did I ever say that you do not love God?" said I gently.

"Well then," said Mr. Gear, "I say it. There is no use in beating about the bush. I say it. I honor him, and revere him, and try to obey him, but I do not particularly love him. I do not know much about him. I do not feel toward him as I want my children to feel toward me. What would you have me do Mr. Laicus? Would you have me play the hypocrite? God has got flatterers enough. I do not care to swell their number."

"I would have you honest with him as you are with me," I replied. "I would have you kneel down, and tell him what you have told me; tell him that you do not know him, and ask him that you may; tell him that you do not love him and ask him that you may."

"You orthodox people," said he, "say that no man can come to God with an unregenerate heart; and mine is an unregenerate heart. At least I suppose so. I have been told so often enough. You tell us that no man can come that has not been convicted and converted. I have never suffered conviction or experienced conversion. I cannot cry out to God, "God be merciful to me a sinner." For I don't believe I am a sinner. I don't pretend to be perfect. I get out of temper now and then. I am hard on my children sometimes, was on Willie to-night, poorly fellow. I even rip out an oath occasionally. I am sorry for that habit and mean to get the better of it yet. But I can't make a great pretence of sorrow that I do not experience."

"You have lived," said I, "for over thirty years the constant recipient of God's mercies and loving kindnesses, and never paid him the poor courtesy of a thank you. You have trespassed on his patience and his love in ways innumerable through all these thirty years, and never said so much as I beg pardon. And now you can look back upon it all and feel no sorrow. I am sorry if it is so, Mr. Gear. But if it is, it need not keep you from your God. You can be at least as frank with him as you have been with me. You can tell him of your indifference if you can not tell him of your penitence or your love."

There was a pause.

"You believe in prayer," I continued. "You are indignant that I suspected you of disbelief; and yet you never pray. Are you not living without God; is it not true of you that 'God is not in all your thoughts?'"

He was silent.

"Will you turn over a new leaf in your lifebook?" said I. "Will you commence this night a life of prayer?"

He shook his head very slightly, almost imperceptibly. "I will make no promises," said he. But still he spoke more to himself than to me.

"Mr. Gear," said I, "is it not evident that it is no use for you and me to discuss theology? It is not a difference of doctrine that separates us. Here is a fundamental duty; you acknowledge it, you assert its importance, but you have never performed it; and now that your attention is called to it you will not even promise to fulfil it in the future."

"Mr. Laicus," said he, "I will think of it. Perhaps you are right. I have always meant to do my duty, if my duty was made clear. Perhaps I have failed, failed possibly in a point of prime importance. I do not know. I am in a maze. I believe there is a knowledge of God that I do not possess, a love of God that I do not experience. I believe in it because I believe in you M. Laicus, and yet more because I believe in my wife. But may be it will come in time. Time works wonders."

My very words to Jennie. And Jennie's answer was mine to him.

"Time never works Mr. Gear. It eats, and undermines, and rots, and rusts, and destroys. But it never works. It only gives us an opportunity to work."

And so I came away.

CHAPTER XVII.
Wanted--A Pastor.

WE are in a sorry condition here at Wheathedge. The prospects are, that it will be worse before it is better. For weeks now (it seems like a year or two) we have been without the Gospel. I do not mean that literally the preaching of the Gospel has been dispensed with. On the contrary, I have heard more sermons on the text, "I am determined to know nothing among you save Jesus Christ, and Him crucified," than I ever heard before in my life. We are hearing candidates, and every candidate seems to feel it necessary to declare himself, to propound a sort of religious platform. The sermons seem to me to have about as much relation, as a general thing, to the spiritual condition of the hearers as Gov. Hoffman's last message to the real interests of the people of the State. In fact, if the truth were told, it is not a sermon we want, but a platform. We invite the candidate to preach, not that we may profit by the Gospel, but that he may show us his face. It has become a psychological curiosity to see how many different sermons can be evolved from that one text. I wonder sometimes if St. Paul would know himself in his modern attire.

I am very glad that Maurice Mapleson did not accept my invitation to come to Wheathedge, to preach as a candidate. For listening to a candidate and listening to the Gospel are two very different things. The candidate preaches to show us how he can do it. We listen to hear how he can do it. From the moment he enters the pulpit all eyes are fixed upon him. His congregation is all attention. Let him not flatter himself. It is as critics, not as sinners, that we listen. We turn round to see how he walks up the aisle. Is his wife so unfortunate as to accompany him? We analyze her bonnet, her dress, her features, her figure. If not, he monopolizes all attention. In five minutes we can, any of us-there are a few rare exceptions-tell you the cut of his coat, the character of his cravat, the shape of his collar, the way he wears his hair. If he has any peculiar pulpit habit, woe betide him; he is odd. If he has not, woe betide him; he is commonplace and conventional. He rises to invoke the blessing of God. If he goes to the throne of God he goes alone. We go no farther than the pulpit. We tell one another afterwards that he is eloquent in prayer, or that his prayers are very common. If his style is solemn, we condemn him as stilted. If it is conversational, we condemn him as too colloquial and familiar. He reads a hymn. We compare his elocution with that of our own favorites, or with some imaginary ideal, if we have no favorites. He preaches. We can, any of us, tell you how he does it. But what he says, there are not half a dozen who can tell. Does he tell us of our sins? We do not look at our own hearts, but at his picture, to see if it is painted well. Does he hold before us the cross? We do not bow before it. We ask, is it well carved and draped? The Judgment is only a dramatic poem; the Crucifixion only a tableau.

So, though we have preaching, we have no Gospel at Wheathedge.

Perhaps the lack of the parish is quite as painfully felt in other departments as in the pulpit. The Church is without a head. It flounders about like a headless chicken; excuse the homely simile, which has nothing but truth to commend it. When Mrs. Beale died last week, we had to send to Wheatensville to get a minister to attend the funeral. When Sallie D. was married she sent there, too, for a minister. He was out of town, and the ceremony came near being delayed a week for want of him. The prayer-meeting lags. Little coldnesses between church members break out into open quarrels. There is no one to weld the dissevered members. Poor old Mother Lang, who has not left her bed for five years, laments bitterly her loss, and asks me every time I call to see her, "When will you get a pastor?" The Young People's Association begins to droop. Even the Sunday-school shows signs of friction, though Deacon Goodsole succeeds in keeping it in tolerably good running order by his imperturbable good humor. One advantage we have gained by this interregnum-only one. Even Mr. Hardcap is convinced that pastoral labors are not so unimportant as he had imagined.

For myself, I am in despair. I made no very serious objection to being put on the supply committee. I fancied the task a comparatively easy one. I had understood that there was no lack of ministers wanting places. There is none. We have applications three or four deep, of all sorts and kinds, from parishless clergymen. But such a jury as the Wheathedge congregation affords, I never saw and hope never to see again. I only wish there was some law to treat them as other juries are treated: shut them up in the jury-room till they agree on a verdict.

The first minister was too old; he would not suit the young folks. The second, just out of the seminary, was too young; the old folks said he had not experience. The third had experience. He had been in a parish three years. He was still young, with the elastic hopes and strong enthusiasm of youth. But he was a bachelor. The people pretty universally declared that the minister should have a wife and a house. The women all said there must be somebody to organize the sewing circles, and to lead the female prayer-meetings. The fourth was married, but he had three or four children. We could not support him. The fifth was a most learned man, who told us the original Greek or Hebrew of his texts, and, morning or evening, never came nearer to America than Rome under Augustus C'sar. He was dull. The sixth afforded us a most brilliant pyrotechnic display. He spluttered, and fizzed, and banged, as though Fourth of July himself had taken orders and gone to preaching. The young people were carried away. But the old folks all said he was sensational.

Then, besides those we have heard, there are several we have talked about. There is the Rev. Mr. C-- who has the reputation of being a most excellent pastor. He is indefatigable in visiting the sick, in comforting the afflicted, in dealing with the recreant and the unconverted. But Mr. Wheaton says emphatically he will never do for our people. "He is no preacher, Mr. Laicus," says he; "and our people demand first-rate preaching. We must have a man that can draw."

We talked over Mr. K--. He is a rare preacher, by all accounts. I understand that his health has suffered somewhat by excessive study, and he would like another parish, a quieter one, where he can have more time to his study, and can use his old sermons. He preached once or twice in exchange with our old pastor before he left. But Solomon Hardcap would not hear of him, and even Deacon Goodsole shook his head at his suggestion, "He is not social," said the Deacon. "He does not know half the people in Highkrik, where he has been settled for over five years. He often passes his best friend without noticing him, on the street." "Never would do," says Mr. Hardcap. "He only visits his people once a year. I want to know my minister. We want a man who will run in and out as though he cared for us. Preaching is all very well, but we don't want a minister who is all talk."

I am in despair. And despite the breach of ecclesiastical etiquette, I have resolved to resort to advertising. I have not submitted my advertisement to the other members of the committee, but I am sure that it is in accord with the general feelings of the Church.

"Jennie, what do you think of my sending this advertisement to the Christian Union?"

WANTED.-A pastor. He must be irreproachable in his dress, without being an exquisite; married, but without children, young, but with great experience; learned, but not dull; eloquent in prayer, without being colloquial or stilted; reverential, but not conventional; neither old nor commonplace; a brilliant preacher, but not sensational; know every one, but have no favorites; settle all disputes, engage in none; be familiar with the children, but always dignified; be a careful writer, a good extempore speaker, and an assiduous and diligent pastor. Such a person, to whom salary is less an object than a "field of usefulness," may hear of an advantageous opening by addressing Wheathedge, care of "The Christian Union," 27, Park Place.

CHAPTER XVIII.
Our Prayer-Meeting.

ONE thing we have gained by losing our pastor-the promise of better prayer-meetings.

Not that he was recreant in his duty. He performed it only too well. We learned to depend on him. He suffered us to do so. It was only by a delicate irony that the prayer-meeting could be termed one of the "social meetings" of the Church. A solemn stillness pervaded the room. No one ever spoke after he entered the awful presence, unless he rose, formally addressed "the chair," and delivered himself of a set address. Occasionally one bolder than the rest spoke in a sepulchral whisper to his neighbor-that was all. In other social meetings the ladies, according to my observation, bear their full burden of conversation. In our prayer-meetings no woman ever ventured to open her mouth. In fact, I hardly know why they were called prayer-meetings. We rarely had any greater number of prayers than in our usual Sabbath service. Yes, I think we usually had one more.

The minister entered solemnly at the appointed hour, walked straight to his desk, without a word, a bow, a smile of recognition; read a long hymn, offered a very respectable imitation of the "long prayer," gave out a second hymn, and called on an elder to pray, who always imitated the imitation, and included in his broad sympathies all that his pastor had just prayed for-the Church, the Sabbath-school, the unconverted, backsliders, those in affliction, the President and all those in authority, the (Presbyterian) bishops and other clergy, not forgetting the heathen and the Jews. Then followed a passage of Scripture for a text from the pastor, with a short sermon thereafter. Nor was it always short. I fancied he felt the necessity of occupying the time. It was not unfrequently long enough for a very respectable discourse, if length gives the discourse its respectability. Then we had another prayer from another layman, and then the invariable announcement, "the meeting is now open," and the invariable result, a long, dead pause. In fact, the meeting would not open. Like an oyster, it remained pertinaciously shut. Occasionally some good elder would rise to break the painful silence, by repeating some thought from the previous Sunday's sermon, or by telling some incident or some idea which he had seen in a previous number of "The Christian Union." But as we had all been to church, and as most of us take "The Christian Union," this did not add much to the interest of the meeting. Generally another prayer and hymn, sometimes two, sufficed to fill the hour. The pastor kept his eye on the clock. When the hand pointed to nine he rose for the benediction. And never did a crowd of imprisoned schoolboys show more glad exultation at their release than was generally indicated by these brethren and sisters when the words of benediction dismissed them from their period of irksome restraint. Every man, and every woman, too, found a tongue. We broke up into little knots. A busy hum of many voices replaced the dead silence. The "social meeting" commenced when the "prayer-meeting" ended. This, I think, is a fair portraiture of our prayer-meetings at Wheathedge as they were during our late pastor's presence with us.

The fault was not his-at least it was only proximately his. He felt the burden, groaned under it, tried hard, poor man! to remedy the evil. He often came to consult me about it. He tried various plans. He gave a course of weekly lectures. The prayer-meeting was less a meeting of prayer than before. No man was willing to follow his elaborate lecture with a fragmentary talk. He announced from the pulpit, the preceding Sabbath, the topic for the next meeting. Worse and worse! A few members conscientiously studied up the passage in "Barnes's Notes" and the "Comprehensive Commentary," and brought us the result of their investigations in discourse powerfully prosy, and recondite with second hand learning. The Minister at last gave up the matter in despair. I think the condition of our prayer-meetings was one consideration which greatly influenced him in deciding to leave.

I thought that there was nothing left in them to be lost, that no change could be other than for the better; but after he went what little meeting we had fell away. The few who had been attracted by his personal presence ceased to come. In vain we endeavored to revive our flagging spirits by continually reminding one another that the promise was to two or three gathered together. That was our standard text. Every leader referred to it in his prayers, and generally in his opening remarks. We had need of it. For the last two weeks there were not members enough present to serve as pall-bearers for the dead prayer-meeting.

This brought about a crisis. Two weeks ago, Deacon Goodsole came to me to talk over the spiritual condition of our church. I agreed with him that the prayer-meeting was a fatal symptom if not a fatal disease. We agreed to do what we could to remedy it. We asked the session to put it into our hands. They were only too glad to do so. We spoke quietly to two other of the brethren to co-operate with us. We divided the parish among ourselves, and undertook to visit all the praying and waking members-not a very onerous task. We talked with one by one, concerning the spiritual condition of the church, asked them to come next week to the prayer-meeting, and to bring with them warm hearts. "Come," we said, "from your closets. Come in the spirit of prayer." Fifteen minutes before the hour of meeting we four met in the Bible-class room. One agreed to act that night as leader. It was Deacon Goodsole. He told the rest of us his subject. Then we all knelt together and asked God's blessing on our prayer-meeting. From that brief and simple conference we went together to the conference-room. Each one agreed to carry some offering with him-a word, a prayer, a hymn. Each one agreed also to bring in speech but a single thought, and in prayer but a single petition. The leader himself should occupy but five minutes. Our hearts were aglow. We never had such a prayer-meeting in Wheathedge. Deacon Goodsole did not have to announce that the prayer-meeting was open. It opened itself. We had hard work to close it. The meeting last week was preceded in the same manner by fifteen minutes of prayer. It was characterized by the same warmth and freshness. We are astonished to find how short our hour is when we come to the meeting from our knees, when we bring to it, in our hearts, the spirit of God. We have no long speeches. So far we have had few exhortations and much true experience. Shall we fall back again into the old ruts? Perhaps. It is something that we are not in them now. Meanwhile, from this brief experience I cull five proverbs for my own reflection.

The minister cannot make a good meeting.

Warm hearts are better than great thoughts.

Solemn faces do not make sacred hours.

Little leading makes much following.

Brevity is the soul of the prayer-meeting.

CHAPTER XIX.
We are Jilted.

WHEATHEDGE is in a fever of excitement-not very agreeable excitement. Disappointment and anger are curiously commingled. Little knots of men and women gathered after church on Sunday in excited discussion. A by-stander might overhear in these conferences such phrases dropped as "Shameful." "It's too bad." "If he is that sort of man it's very fortunate we did not get him." "I have no faith in ministers," and the like. Do you ask what is the matter? We have been jilted.

I will not give names, at least not the true ones. For I have no inclination to involve myself in a newspaper controversy, and none to injure the prospects of a young man who possesses qualities which fit him for abundant usefulness if vanity and thoughtlessness do not make shipwreck of him.

For six months now we have been without a pastor. We are hard to suit. Mr. Wheaton was right. Wheathedge is a peculiar place, and requires a very peculiar man. But about six weeks ago there came along a very peculiar man. He seemed to be just adapted to the place. He was fresh from the seminary. He had a wife but no children. He was full of enthusiasm. As a preacher he was free from conventionalism, bright, sparkling, brilliant; more brilliant than warm. In private life he was social, genial, unministerial. Old Aunt Sue did indeed complain that when he called there he did not offer to pray with her. And good old Father Haines said he wished that there was less poetry and more Christ in his sermons. But neither old Aunt Sue nor old Father Haines contribute much to the support of the Church, and their criticisms did nothing to abate the general enthusiasm. Jim Wheaton said he was just the man, and promised to double his subscription, if necessary, to get him. Deacon Goodsole was scarcely less enthusiastic. I do not think there was a dissenting voice among the ladies; and the young folks were absolutely unanimous.

"If we can only get Mr. Uncannon," said Jim Wheaton to me one morning, as we rode to the city in the cars together, "in three weeks we will drain the Methodist church dry of its young folks."

Personally, I have no taste for foraging in other men's fields. But I knew that

Jim Wheaton would not appreciate my sentiments, and so I kept silence.

Mr. Uncannon preached for us two Sabbaths. He spent the intervening week in Wheathedge. He visited with Deacon Goodsole most of the leading families. He stopped at Mr. Wheaton's. If the people had been charmed with him in pulpit they were delighted with him in the parlor. The second Sabbath I do not think there would have been a dissenting voice to the call.

There was only one difficulty. It was considered very doubtful if we could get him. That doubt I undertook to solve.

Monday he returned to the city. I went down in the same train, and took occasion to fall into conversation with him. I told him frankly the state of feeling. I represented that it was very desirable that the matter should go no further unless there was a prospect that he would consider favorably a call if it were given him. He replied with equal frankness. He said that he was delighted with the place and with the people. He wanted to come. There was only one obstacle. He understood that we paid our former pastor only $1,200 a year. He could not undertake to live on that.

"In fact," said he, "they want me very much at North Bizzy, in Connecticut. They pay there $1,500 a year. It is a manufacturing town. I do not think either the society or the work would be as congenial as in Wheathedge. I like the quiet of your rural parish. I appreciate the advantages it would afford me for study. But $300 is a good deal of money. I do not want to be mercenary, Mr. Laicus, but I do not want to be pinched."

I assured him that no such difficulty should stand in his way. When I returned, I found he had expressed the same sentiments to Deacon Goodsole and Mr. Wheaton. We were all agreed that we would do as well as North Bizzy. So we gave him a call at $1,500. Possibly we presumed too much; but we generally considered it as good as settled.

The Sabbath after the call he came to Wheathedge. This time he brought his young wife with him. The ladies were more charmed than ever. All Wheathedge turned out to see and hear our new minister. He remained over to our weekly prayer-meeting. It was astonishing what a spirit of devotion was awakened in our church. I have never seen the prayer-meeting so fully attended. He seemed fully to reciprocate our enthusiasm. He and his wife were tireless in the praises of the beauties of Wheathedge. "It is just the place," said Mrs. Uncannon, "in which I should choose to spend my days." Of course this saying was repeated all over the parish, and this evidence of her appreciative taste increased very measurably her own and her husband's popularity.

He went away Thursday morning without giving a final and definite answer. Deacon Goodsole indeed asked him point blank for one. He replied that though his mind was about made up, still he felt that so solemn a connection ought not to be made without a prayerful consideration. This was all very proper. We waited, with patience, till this decorous delay should be over. But we already considered him our pastor.

It was the next week that Deacon Goodsole came into my house one evening, in a state of great excitement. He had an open letter in his hand. "Look there," said he. "The Church at North Bizzy is trying to get our minister away from us."

The letter was from Mr. Uncannon. It was to the effect that the Church at North Bizzy were taking measures to secure a parsonage. He preferred to come to Wheathedge, but he did not know what he should do for a house. There had been, he believed, some talk of building a parsonage at Wheathedge. He felt very desirous to take his bride to her "home"--not to depend on boarding-houses or landlords. If this could be provided he thought it would settle the question; for both he and his wife infinitely preferred the clear air and sunny skies, and grand old mountains, and glorious river basking in the golden sunlight, &c., &c., to the dust and soot and noise of man's busy but dirty industry.

"Very well," said I. "I do not care to bid against the Church at North Bizzy. But I have always wanted a parsonage at Wheathedge. I will be one of five to pay the rent for this year, and one of ten to build one next year."

Deacon Goodsole started a subscription paper on the spot. In a few days we had secured a house for the year, and money enough to make our building operation certain. The Deacon wrote Mr. Uncannon accordingly. We expected his answer forthwith, and his arrival soon after. Wheathedge was at last satisfied.

Imagine, then, if you can, the chagrin and disappointment which was caused when, last Sunday morning, a letter was read from Mr. Uncannon to Mr. James Wheaton, Chairman of the Board of Trustees, declining the call. Mr. Uncannon had given it his most prayerful consideration. He was deeply moved by the warm welcome which had been accorded to him. He had hoped that the Lord would make it plain that it was to be his privilege to cast in his lot with us. But the Lord had ordered it otherwise. The Providential indications seemed to him clear that it was his duty to labor in another field.

But he united his prayers with ours that the Great Bishop would soon send us a pastor who should feed us with the bread of life.

Deacon Goodsole says that the Providential indications are a salary of $1,800 and a parsonage; and Mr. Wheaton says if any other young man succeeds in playing us off against a rival parish he is mistaken; that's all. Even gentle Jennie is indignant. "Of all flirtation, ministerial flirtation seems to me to be the worse," she says; and truth to tell, she never had much patience with any other.

I do not want to judge Mr. Uncannon too harshly. In fact I am not in a very judicial frame of mind. But, whatever his intent, his ministerial coquetry has injured the cause of Christ in Wheathedge more than a year of preaching can benefit it in North Bizzy. Meanwhile, the parsonage, which we hired, lies vacant on our hands, and waits for an occupant.

CHAPTER XX.
We propose.

WE are in the valley of humiliation. Since the church has been rejected, it has an opportunity to understand how a candidate feels when he is rejected. I am inclined on consideration to recall the last paragraph of the last chapter. I am inclined to think Mr. Uncannon may prove a "means of grace" to us yet. He has certainly been a thorn in the side.

On further consideration, I do retract it. I here emphatically record that first thoughts are not always best thoughts, and that it is my sober second judgment that Mr. Uncannon has done us more good than he has the parish at North Bizzy. We gave him to them grudgingly. But it has been a case in which the proverb applies: It is more blessed to give than to receive. For Mr. Uncannon's flirtation has probably given us Maurice Mapleson for a pastor.

Two weeks ago I was coming up from New York on the train. Deacon Goodsole was in the seat in front of me. My satchel was my only traveling companion. And I, according to custom, was enjoying a train nap, when I was aroused by a hand on my shoulder coupled with a hearty "Hallo! you could not be sounder asleep if you were in church and Dr. Argure was in the pulpit."

It was Mr. Wheaton.

"Good afternoon," said I. "Sit down." And my satchel exchanged its seat for a place in my lap in order to make room for Mr. Wheaton on the seat beside me.

"Look here, gentlemen," said Mr. Wheaton, taking the proffered seat, "we've been fooling about this minister business long enough."

"Been fooled you mean," said Deacon Goodsole.

"I tell you," said Mr. Wheaton, slapping his knee by way of emphasis, "that young Maurice Mapleson is the man for us. The more I think of it the more I am sure of it."

"He is a right earnest man," said the Deacon. "I think he was the first spark we have seen in the ashes of our prayer meeting for many a day."

"Can't you get him to come down, Mr. Laicus?" asked Mr. Wheaton.

I shook my head resolutely.

"Not as a candidate you know, but on some dodge or other. Invite him to spend a week with you, and book on to him for the pulpit when Sunday comes."

"He isn't the man for dodges," said the Deacon, doubtfully.

I shook my head as decidedly to the second proposition as to the first.

"Well then," said Mr. Wheaton, "if he won't come here we will have to go there. It isn't far."

The Deacon doubted whether the church would agree to deviate from the old paths.

"They wouldn't have done it," said Mr. Wheaton. "But they'll agree to anything now I think."

"Mr. Gear recommended that plan when we first met," said I. "He will approve of it. But how as to Mr. Hardcap?"

"Oh! no matter about Hardcap," said Mr. Wheaton, "he's no account."

"Excuse me," said I, "he is one of our committee and is of account."

So after some consultation it was finally agreed that we should get off at the Mill Village Station to see Mr. Gear, and then walk up to Wheathedge. Deacon

Goodsole also proposed to put Mr. Hardcap on the special committee to go to Koniwasset Corners, and Mr. Wheaton said he would furnish a free pass over the road to all who would go. No man is impervious to compliments if they are delicately administered. At all events Mr. Gear was sensibly pleased by having us call on him in a body. And Mr. Hardcap, when he found that the new plan involved a free ride on the railroad and a Sunday excursion for himself, withdrew all objections.

My wife says, "For shame, John," and wants me to strike that last sentence out. But it is true, and I do not know why it should not stand. It is in confidence you know.

The next Saturday Mr. Wheaton, Mr. Hardcap and Deacon Goodsole started for Koniwasset Corners. They reached it, or rather they reached Koniwasset, the nearest point, Saturday evening, and Sunday morning rode over, a drive of five miles. It was a beautiful day; the congregation turned out well; the little church was full, and Maurice, unconscious of the presence of a committee, and preaching, not to fish for a place, but to fish for men, was free, unconstrained and, as Providence willed it, or as good fortune would have it (the reader may have his choice of expressions, according as he is Christian or heathen), was in a good mood. Deacon Goodsole was delighted. Jim Wheaton was scarcely less so, and even Mr. Hardcap was pleased to say that it was "a real plain Gospel sermon." Deacon Goodsole found an old friend in one of the congregation and went home with him to dinner, while Mr. Wheaton and Mr. Hardcap went back to the hotel. Deacon Goodsole joined them in the evening and brought a good report of the Sunday-school, where he had watched the unconscious parson (who superintends his own school), and had even, to avoid suspicion, taken the place of an absent teacher for the afternoon.

Mr. Wheaton had to return the next day, but the Deacon found no great difficulty in persuading Mr. Hardcap to stay over, and Tuesday evening they went to the weekly prayer-meeting. Meanwhile they inquired quietly in the neighborhood about the preacher at the Corners, giving however no one a hint of their object, except the parson at Koniwasset who commended Maurice very highly for his piety and his efficiency. As to his preaching, he said he should not call him eloquent, "but" he added, "there is one thing; Maurice Mapleson never speaks without having something to say; and he is very much in earnest."

Both the Deacon and Mr. Hardcap were very much pleased with the spirit of the prayer-meeting--the Deacon said Mr. Mapleson could make more of a fire with less fuel than any man he knew--and when the committee made their report, which they did at the close of our Wednesday evening meeting, it was unanimous in favor of giving Maurice a call.

To call a man without hearing him was not the orthodox way, and the objections which Mr. Hardcap had originally proposed in the committee meeting were renewed by others. In reply it was said, very truly, that the church really knew more about Mr. Mapleson than they could possibly learn from a trial sermon, or even from half a dozen of them, that a careful investigation by a committee into his actual working power was a far better test than any pulpit exhibition, however brilliant. I added that Mapleson's letter was positive, and his convictions settled, and that I felt reasonably certain he would not preach as a candidate. On the whole this increased the desire to get him; and finally a second committee was appointed to go and hear him. A couple of ladies were put, informally, on this committee, and the church paid the expenses of the four. I say informally. Deacon Goodsole nominated Miss Moore and Mrs. Biskit, and quoted the case of Phoebe from the sixteenth chapter of Romans to prove that it was apostolic. But the ladies shook their heads, as did some of the elders of the church and Mr. Hardcap entered a vigorous protest. The Deacon was a born and bred Congregationalist, and is radical, I am afraid, in church matters. A compromise was finally effected by appointing two of the elders, who agreed to take their wives.

They came back as well pleased as the first committee had been, and the result was, to make a long story short, that last week a unanimous call was sent to Maurice, and as I write this letter I have before me a private note from him, saying that he has received it, and that, if agreeable to us, he will come down and spend a week with me. He says he wants to see our prayer-meeting, our Sabbath-school teachers' meeting, and our Sabbath-school. He adds that he will preach for us on Sunday if we desire, but that he does not want it known that he will be here at the prayer-meeting, as he wants to take a back seat and see how it goes.

In short he gives me to understand that it is the church which is on trial, not the minister, and that whether he comes or not depends on what kind of a church he finds it to be. This reversal of the ordinary course of things is a little queer; but I guess it is all right. At all events it will not do the church at Wheathedge any harm.

Meanwhile until we get a final answer from Maurice Mapleson our pulpit is no longer in the market. For after our experience of ministerial coquetry I do not think there will be any inclination on our part for a flirtation.

CHAPTER XXI.
Ministerial Salaries.

"MR. Wheaton," said I, "we made a queer blunder the other night; we did not settle on any salary when we made out our call to Mr. Mapleson."

"No blunder," said Mr. Wheaton, "I left it out on purpose. I thought may be we could get him for less than fifteen hundred dollars. What do you think? Wouldn't he come on twelve hundred, and the parsonage?" And Mr. Wheaton smiled on me with an air of self-satisfaction which seemed to say, 'Jim Wheaton is the man to manage church business.'

I confess I was indignant at the idea of driving a sharp bargain with a minister, but I rather suspect Jim Wheaton never makes any other than a sharp bargain.

"Not with my advice," said I. "I told him the church ought to pay fifteen hundred a year and a parsonage, and I presumed it would. But I recommend him not to come till he knows."

We were in the Post Office, waiting for the distribution of the evening mail. Mr. Hardcap was one of our group. So was Deacon Goodsole. It was indeed a sort of extemporized and unintentional meeting of our supply committee, only Mr. Gear being absent.

"The church won't give mor'n 1,200 with my advice," said Mr. Hardcap decidedly. "And that's mor'n I make. I would just like to contract my time for the year at four dollars a day. And I have to get up at six and work till sunset, ten hours, hard work. I don't see why the parson should have half as much again for five or six hours' work. I have heard our old pastor say myself that he never allowed himself to study mor'n six hours a day."

"But the pastoral work, Mr. Hardcap?" said I. "You make no account of that."

"The calls, do you mean?" said he. "Well, I should like to be paid four dollars a day for just dressin' up in my best and visitin', that's all."

"Not only the calls," said I, "though you would find calling anything but recreation, if it was your business. But there are the prayer-meetings, and the Sabbath-school, and the whole management and direction of the church."

"Prayer-meetin' and Sabbath-school!" replied Mr. Hardcap; "don't we all work in them? And we don't ask any salary for it. I guess it ain't no harder for the parson to go to prayer-meetin' than for me."

I shrugged my shoulders. The deacon interposed.

"I agree with you, Mr. Laicus," said he. "We have got to pay a good salary. I wish we could make it two thousand a year instead of fifteen hundred."

Mr. Hardcap opened his eyes and pursed his mouth firmly together, as though he would say 'Do my ears deceive me?'

"But," continued the deacon, "there is something in what Mr. Hardcap says. There are half-a-dozen farmers in our Wheathedge congregation who don't handle fifteen hundred dollars in money from one year's end to the other. Mr. Hardcap isn't the only man to whom it seems a big sum to pay. Mr. Lapstone the shoemaker, Mrs. Croily the seamstress, Joe Hodgkins the blacksmith, and half-a-dozen others I could name, have to live on less. And you must remember their incomes, Mr. Laicus, as well as yours, and mine, and Mr. Wheaton's here."

"Well, gentlemen," said Mr. Wheaton, "we've got to pay a good salary, but I think we ought to keep expenses down all we can."

"I don't believe in makin' preachin' a money makin' business no-how," said Mr. Hardcap. "Parsons hain't got no business to be a layin' up of earthly riches, and fifteen hundred dollars is a good deal of money to spend on bread and butter, now I tell you."

"Mr. Hardcap," said I, "what do your tools cost you?"

"My tools?" said he. "Yes," said I, "your tools. What do they cost you?"

"Well," said he, "they range all the way from ten cents up to five dollars, accordin' to the article and its quality."

"Did you ever consider," said I, "what a minister's tools cost?"

"Minister's tools!" said he, "I didn't know he had any, except his pen."

"My dear sir," said I, "his tools alone cost him between one and two hundred dollars a year."

Mr. Hardcap expressed his incredulity by a long whistle; and even Deacon

Goodsole expressed a quiet doubt. But my father was a minister and I know something about it.

"Look here," said I. "He must have at least two religious weeklies, one of his own denomination, and one of a more general character," and I took out a pencil and paper and noted down my list as I made it, "that's six dollars. He ought to have at least two of the popular magazines, that's eight dollars. He ought to have a good scientific magazine of some kind, four dollars more; and his theological quarterly is indispensable, four dollars more; and at least one of the daily newspapers, he ought really to read on both sides, but we will allow only one, that's ten dollars, and here is the footing of his periodical literature: Two religious weeklies $6 Popular Magazines 8 Scientific Magazine 4 Theological Quarterly 4 Daily Paper 10 $32"

"That's what it will cost him," said I, "simply to keep up with the times."

The other gentlemen looked at my figures a moment in silence. Deacon Goodsole was the first to speak. "That is a pretty liberal estimate," said he. "A great many ministers get along on less than that."

"Oh yes," said I, "and grow dry and dull in consequence. Little food makes lean men."

Mr. Hardcap shook his head resolutely, "I don't believe in preachin' to the times," said he. "It's scripter interpretation and the doctrines we want."

"Very well," said I, "the tools for that work cost more yet. Yours cost you from ten cents to five dollars, his from five dollars to a hundred. A single volume of Lange, or Alford, or the Speaker's Commentary cost five dollars; a good Bible Dictionary, from twenty to thirty; a good Encyclopedia, from fifty to a hundred. And theological treaties have a small market and therefore a high price-very high for their value. And his tools grow old too, and have to be replaced oftener than yours do, Mr. Hardcap."

"I don't see that, Mr. Laicus," said he. "A book, if you keep it careful, will last a great many years. I am reading out of a Bible that belonged to my grandfather. And I expect 'll belong to my grandson yet."

"My dear Mr. Hardcap," said I, "the leaves and covers and printed works do not make the book. Ideas make the book. You can use your tools over and over again. If your plane gets dull out comes the hones and the dulled edge is quickly sharpened again. But ideas are gone when they are used."

"I don't see it," said Mr. Hardcap. And I do not suppose he does. I wonder if he knows what an idea is.

"It is so," continued I, "with all student-tools. There are a few which the minister uses over and over again; his dictionaries, commentaries, and cyclopedia, if he has one. There are a few treaties that are worth reading and re-reading; but they are exceptional. Generally the student gets the gist of a book in one reading, as a squirrel the kernel of a nut at one crack. What remains on his shelves thereafter is only a shell. A book that has been dulled can rarely be sharpened and put to use again. There is no ministerial hone. The parson must replenish his bench every year. At least he ought to."

"I haven't no great opinion of larned ministers no-how," said Mr. Hardcap. "It isn't larnin' we want, Mr. Laicus. It is the Gospel, the pure, unadulterated Gospel."

Mr. Hardcap was incorrigible. I might as well try to explain to a North American Indian the cost and the value of a modern cotton mill as the cost and the value of student tools to Mr. Hardcap.

But I believe I produced some impression on the others. Deacon Goodsole still pondered my figures. "I never thought of the cost of minister's tool before," said he. "It's quite an item."

"Well," said Mr. Hardcap, "for my part I don't see why the parson can't live on a thousand dollars a year as well as I can."

I had failed to produce conviction on the subject of tools. I resolved to try another tack. "What do you pay for help?" said I.

"Help?" said he interrogatively.

"Yes," said I. "What do you pay your cook and chambermaid?"

"Hoh!" said he contemptuously. "I don't keep no help. My Bible tells me that God made the wife to be a help-meet for man, and my wife is all the help I want. I wouldn't have a servant round my house at no price."

"Do you suppose our pastor and his wife can get along the same way?" I asked.

"Don't see why not," said he sententiously.

"What!" said Mr. Wheaton. "Would you have your pastor's wife do her own work, Mr. Hardcap? I hope we haven't got so poor as that. She must be a lady, Mr. Hardcap; a lady, sir."

"Well," said Mr. Hardcap, "and can't a lady do her own work? High and mighty notions these that a woman must eat the bread of idleness to be a lady."

"Oh! it's all very well, Mr. Hardcap," said Mr. Wheaton; "but our pastor's wife has a position to maintain. She owes a duty to the parish, sir. She can't be maid of all work at home. I should be ashamed of the church to suffer it."

"There certainly is a difference, Mr. Hardcap," said the Deacon. "Mrs. Hardcap may do her own washing. And if anybody finds her over the washtub Monday morning no one thinks the worse of her for it. But it really wouldn't do for our pastor's wife."

Mr. Hardcap shook his head resolutely. "I don't see it," said he. "I don't believe a minister's wife is too good to work."

"She isn't," said the Deacon. "But if she washes Monday, and irons Tuesday, and sweeps Wednesday, and bakes Thursday, and sews Friday and Saturday, what time has she left to make calls or receive them?"

Mr. Hardcap only shrugged his shoulders.

"How many calls does your wife make in a year?" I asked.

"Oh! we don't make no calls," said Mr. Hardcap. "We've got other work to do."

"And yet you expect your minister and his wife to call on you?" said I interrogatively.

"I s'pose so," said he.

"I remember hearing you say that you thought it rather hard of Mrs. Work, just before they left, that she hadn't been inside of your house for six months. How many calls do you suppose Mrs. Mapleson would have to make in a year in order to call on every family once in six months?"

"Don't know," said Mr. Hardcap, shortly.

"Well," said the Deacon, "we've got over a hundred families in our parish. It would take nearly one call every day."

"Beside extra calls on the sick," I continued. "You will either have to give Mrs. Mapleson a servant or relinquish your expectation of receiving any calls from her; that is very evident."

Mr. Hardcap made no reply.

"There are one or two other items that ought to be considered in deciding what the pastor's salary should be," said a gentle but tremulous voice at my side. I turned about to see the speaker. It was old Father Hyatt, who had joined our group, unperceived.

"I suppose Mr. Hardcap's best broadcloth coat and Mrs. Hardcap's black silk gown last them a good many years. Isn't it so, Mr. Hardcap?"

Mr. Hardcap confessed that it was.

"The minister has to wear broadcloth, Mr. Hardcap, all the week. He must be always in society dress. So must his wife. With the utmost economy their bill for clothes mounts up to a frightful sum. I know, for I have tried it."

"There is something in that," said Mr. Hardcap.

Old Father Hyatt is a great favorite with Mr. Hardcap, as indeed he is with all of us. And no one ever accused Father Hyatt of extravagance.

"I know a city clergyman," continued the old man, "who always preaches in a silk gown, though he is a Congregationalist. 'It saves my coat', said he to me once in explanation. 'I can wear a seedy coat in the pulpit and no one is the wiser.' 'But,' said I, 'how about the silk gown?' 'Oh!' said he, 'the ladies furnish the gown.'"

We laughed at the parson's shrewdness. Even Mr. Hardcap smiled.

"And there are some other items, too, gentlemen," added Father Hyatt, "which I hope you will consider. The churches don't ordinarily know about them. At least they do not consider them. The company item alone is an enormous one. Not once in six months now do I have a friend to pass the night with me. But when I was settled here my spare room always had a guest, and half the time my stable an extra horse. Every benevolent agent, every traveling minister, every canvasser makes straight for the minister's house. He has to keep an inn for the benefit of the parish, and gets no pay for it."

"Cut them off," said Mr. Hardcap. But he said it good naturedly.

"'Given to hospitality,' says the Apostle," replied Father Hyatt.

"Well," said Deacon Goodsole, with a sigh, "we ought to pay the fifteen hundred a year. It's none too much. But I don't see where it's coming from."

"Oh! never you fear," said Mr. Wheaton. "Mr. Mapleson is worth fifteen hundred, and we'll have to pay it. We'll get it somehow. Write him it's fifteen hundred, Mr. Laicus. You'll be safe enough."

With which our informal conference came to an end. But I have not written. I wonder if Jim Wheaton runs the Koniwasset Coal Company, and the Newtown railroad, and the Wheathedge bank on the "somehow" principle. I wish had asked him. I am glad I have no stock in them.

CHAPTER XXII.
Ecclesiastical Financiering.

BUT though I have no stock in the Koniwasset Coal Company or the Newtown railroad or the Wheathedge Bank, I have some in the Calvary Presbyterian Church, and I decidedly object on consideration to carry on that institution on the "somehow" principle. So I intimated as much to Mr. Wheaton the other day, after thinking the whole matter over, and taking counsel with Jennie about it.

"Oh! go ahead," said Mr. Wheaton. "Tell him we'll pay him $1,500 and a parsonage. The church will back you, Mr. Laicus."

"And if the church don't," said I, "will you pay the deficit?"

Mr. Wheaton shook his head, very decidedly. I was equally decided that without a responsible backer I would not "go ahead." So on my demand a meeting of the Board of Trustees was called. The Supply Committee met with them. James Wheaton, Esq., Chairman of the Board of Trustees, was in the chair.

On behalf of the Supply Committee I stated the object for which the Board was convened. The church had hitherto paid $1,200 salary. It was quite inadequate. No one doubted that. It was unreasonable to expect that Maurice Mapleson would come for less than we had offered Mr. Uncannon-$1,500 a year and a parsonage. But in the call, by a strange omission, the church had neglected to mention any salary. The Committee wished to write Mr. Mapleson on the subject. Would the Board sustain us in pledging the church to $1,500 and the parsonage?

Upon this there was an informal expression of opinion all round the Board. Mr. Wheaton led the way. He had no doubt on the subject. We must have a minister, a good minister, a live, wide-awake, practical man. Such men were in demand. If one could not be got for $1,200, we must pay $1,500. That was the way in which he managed railroads; and business was business, whether in church or railroad. Not pretending to be a saint, he naturally took a worldly view of the matter; but he at least tried to conduct worldly matters on equitable principles. It was certainly true that the laborer was worthy of his hire.

So, in substance, said James Wheaton, Esq., Chairman Board of Trustees, etc., etc.; and so, in substance, said they all. Even Mr. Hardcap acquiesced, though with a mild protest against modern extravagance.

"Well, gentlemen," said Mr. Wheaton, "this is just what I expected: yes, let me say, just what I was sure of. In fact, I told Mr. Laicus he might depend on having $1,500 a year; but he was not satisfied with my assurance-he wanted yours I hope he is satisfied."

"Excuse me," said I, "if I seem unreasonable, but I am not satisfied; and I should certainly have been so with Mr. Wheaton's assurance. I never doubted that he was good for $1,500 a year. But, in dealing with a church board, to be frank, I want to know where the money is coming from. Pray, Mr. Treasurer, what was our income last year?"

The Treasurer murmured something about not having his accounts.

"In round numbers," said I.

"Between fourteen and fifteen hundred dollars."

"And our expenses?"

"Not far from eighteen hundred dollars."

"And, pray, how," continued I, "was the deficit made up?"

A part, it appears, was made up by a special subscription, and a part is still due as floating debt, and part went in to increase the mortgage. Perhaps I would remember the meeting in the fall at Mr. Wheaton's house.

I did remember it very well. But I was anxious that the other gentlemen should not forget it.

"And now, gentlemen," said I, "you propose to add three hundred dollars to that annual deficit. Where is the money to come from?"

There was a momentary silence. The question was evidently a new one. Apparently not a member of the Board had considered it. At length one gentleman suggested that we must raise the pew rents. This brought an indignant protest from Deacon Goodsole, who is a strong advocate of the free-pew system.

"Never," said he, "with my consent. Any pew-rent is bad enough. Trafficking in the Gospel is abominable at best. It shuts out the poor. Worse than that, it shuts out the godless, the irreligious, the profane--the very men we want to catch. The pew-rents are too high now. We must not raise them."

The Treasurer also added a mild protest. The pew-holders would not stand it.

"What do you say, Mr. Wheaton?" said I.

"Say?" said he: "why, I say you cannot carry on a church on the same principles on which you carry on a railroad or a bank. It is a different affair altogether. You must trust the Lord for something. I think that we can safely trust Him to the amount of three hundred dollars at least. Where's your faith?"

"Making false promises and trusting the Lord to fulfil them isn't faith," said Deacon Goodsole.

"I say, Jim," said Mr. Jowett, "you trust Him for your interest money--that will set us all right."

There was a little laugh at this suggestion. Mr. Wheaton holds a mortgage on the church. He did not take kindly to this practical application of the doctrine of faith.

"Oh! well," said he, "we can raise it somehow. Never fear. A good minister will fill up our empty pews. Then in the summer we must manage to bleed the boarders a little more freely. It won't hurt them. What with a concert, or fair, or a subscription, or a little extra effort our plate collections, we can manage it, I have no doubt."

"For my part," said I, "I agree with one the gentlemen, who told us early in this discussion that we must carry on church affairs on business principles. I don't see any business principles in agreeing to pay money which we have not got and don't know where to get."

"Gentlemen," said Mr. Jowett, "Mr. Laicus is right. The shamefully loose ways in which our Protestant churches carry on their finances is a disgrace to the Christian religion."

Mr. Jowett is a broker. He assured me after the meeting that it was almost impossible to get a loan on church property because churches were so notoriously slack in paying their interest.

Mr. Hardcap murmured an assent. "I don't b'lieve, gentlemen, in agreein' to pay what we hain't got. If we'd got the $1,500, I'd say give it to him. I don't grudge him the money. But I don't want this church to make no promises that it aint' a goin' to keep."

"Mr. Hardcap has had some experience with promise-breaking churches," said Deacon Goodsole.

It seems that Mr. Hardcap did the carpenter work in some repairs on the Methodist church here last summer. When he got through he carried in his bill to the President of the Board of Trustees. The President referred him to the Treasurer. The Treasurer reported no funds and referred him to the Chairman of the Building Committee. The Chairman of the Building Committee explained that it was his business to supervise the building, not to raise the funds, and sent him back to the President. It was not till Mr. Hardcap, whose stock of patience is small, threatened the church with a mechanic's lien that the remedy was forthcoming.

"Well, gentlemen," said I, "I will not be a party to getting a minister here on-excuse the term,--false pretences; on the assurance that we can pay him S1,500 a year when it is a hard matter to pay him $1,200. There are ten of us here. I will put my name down now for $30, if the rest will do the same. If the Lord sends the $300, or if the ladies raise it by a fair, or if Mr. Wheaton gets up a concert, or the summer boarders come to our rescue, we shall have nothing to pay. If none of these things happen, the minister will not have it all to lose."

The matter was eventually settled in that way. We raised a contingent fund of $250 then and there, which we have since made up to $400. So that now we can offer $1,500 a year with a clear conscience.

As a lawyer I have had some experience dealing with corporations. And I record my deliberate conviction here that of all corporations church corporations are financially the worst; the most loose and dilatory and unconsciously dishonest. I record it as my deliberate conviction, having had some opportunities for knowing, that in the Calvinistic church, of the others I don't pretend to know anything, on the average not one half the ministry get their meagre salaries promptly. This injustice is the greatest and most scandalous feature in the treatment to which the churches subject their ministers. That ministers are subjected to hardships is a matter of no consequence. So are other people. It is the injustice, the absolute and indefensible injustice, the promising to pay their meagre salaries and then not paying even those-the obtaining of their services under false pretences-that I complain of. If I were a minister I never would accept a call without knowing thoroughly the income and the expenditure of the church.

As I write there lies before me a letter from my late pastor. He wants to borrow $300 for a few weeks. His Board of Trustees are thus much behind-hand in the first quarter's payment. He has not the means to pay his rent. The duty of the Board in such a case is very evident. The very least they can do is to share in providing temporarily for the exigency. The very most which a mean Board could do would be to ask the minister to unite with them in paying up the deficiency. In fact, he who is least able to do it has to carry it all. Nobody else will trust the church. He has to trust it for hundreds of dollars. And then when his grocer and his landlord and his tailor go unpaid, men shrug their shoulders and say, pityingly, "Oh! he's a minister, he is not trained to business habits." And the world looks on in wonder and in silent contempt to see the Christian Church carrying on its business in a manner the flagrant dishonesty of which would close the doors of any bank, deprive any insurance company of its charter, and drive any broker in Wall street from the Brokers' Board.

Jennie says this last is pretty sharp writing; and she shakes her head over it. But it is time, and I decline to cancel it.

CHAPTER XXIII.
Our Donation Party--by Jane Laicus.

MY husband wants me to write an account of the donation we gave our new minister. He wants it to put in his book.

"Why, John," said I, "I can't write anything for a book. I never wrote anything for print in my life. You mustn't think I am clever because you are."

"My dear Jennie," said he, "there is no magic in print. Write just such an account as you wrote your mother. If you had that letter you could not do better than give me that to put in."

"I can't possibly write, John. I would indeed if I could."

"Then," said John, "it can't go in at all. For I was not here. I cannot describe it."

He was so earnest about it I finally had to yield. He says I always have my own way. I didn't this time I am sure. There is only one thing that reconciles me to it. I do not believe the publishers will print it. I told John I wouldn't trust my writing to his judgment. I wouldn't you know, of course because he would be sure to say it was good. So we agreed to leave it to the publishers. If they don't like this chapter they are going to leave it out. John is going to leave them to read the proof, and we shan't either of us know till the book is published whether "our donation party" gets in or not. I confess to a little hope it will get in.

Let me see how it happened. Oh! this was the way: Maurice was at our house the Sunday he supplied our pulpit. He told my husband that he thought he should accept our call. But he said he didn't think the parsonage would do him any good. He wanted to go to housekeeping, but he had not the money to furnish it with, and he would not run in debt.

That set me thinking. I talked the matter over with Miss Moore and found she was quite of my mind; and the week after, we got Maurice's letter accepting the call, we proposed to the ladies at the sewing society to undertake to furnish the parsonage. The idea took at once. In fact the having a parsonage is a new thing at Wheathedge, and we feel a little pride in having it respectable, you know; at least so as not to be a disgrace to the church. Mrs. Goodsole thought it doubtful about rais-ing the money, and Mrs. Hardcap said that "her husband wasn't in favor of the par-sonage nohow, and she didn't believe would think much of fixin' of it up;" but Miss Moore replied to Mrs. Goodsole that she could try at any rate, and to Mrs. Hardcap that she would be responsible that Mr. Hardcap would do his share; a remark which to some of us seemed a bold one, but which pleased Mrs. Hardcap for all that.

Mr. Hardcap, I believe, means well, though to some of us his ideas do seem very contracted, sometimes. But my husband says that narrow men are needed as well as broad ones, and that if there were no Mr. Hardcap to count the cost of every ven-ture before it was undertaken, the church would have been bankrupt long before this time.

We appointed committees that evening; one to raise the money-of course Miss Moore was at the head of that--one to furnish the kitchen, one to furnish the par-lor and bed-room, (as I knew the bride, I was put on that committee,) and one to provide a supper. Some of the ladies wanted to have a grand reception. They said it would be a good thing to surprise the new pastor with a house-warming. Mrs. Hardcap proposed that the sewing society meet there that afternoon. But Miss

Moore objected strongly. She said it would cost nearly as much to provide a supper for the whole congregation as to furnish a good bed-room set. I think, though, it was really little Miss Flidgett who put a quietus on that plan.

"Why," said she in an injured tone, "I want to be there and see how they like it."

Nobody dared advocate the plan after that speech. I really think that they all felt very much the same way, however.

The next day some of us met at the parsonage to take a survey. Last year the house was without a tenant, and it had come to be in rather a dilapidated condition. The fence gate was off the hinges. The garden was over-grown with weeds. The sink in the kitchen was badly rotted. One of the parlor blinds was off. There was a bad leak over the back porch, and the plastering looked just ready to fall, and the whole looked dingy,--it needed outside painting sadly.

"We needn't let these things go so," said Miss Moore. "The landlord must put the house to rights."

So off we posted to the landlord, who is a queer, crusty old bachelor, who has, I verily believe, a kind heart, and does a good deal of good in his own fashion; but his fashion is never like any one else's. Not a thing could Miss Moore get out of him. He had rented the house as it stood, he said. If the trustees didn't like it they needn't have taken it. They paid little enough rent to repair it themselves. He had nothing more to do except to get his rent regularly, and that she might depend he would do.

Miss Moore returned somewhat disappointed, but nothing daunted. "So much the better," said she. "It will give Mr. Hardcap a chance to do something."

"How about the painting?" said Mrs. Wheaton. "It ought to be painted."

Miss Moore shook her head. "So it ought," she said, "and so I told Mr. Quirk; but he won't do anything,--and we can't afford to paint it; we shouldn't have money left for furnishing."

So we took the measure of the floors for the carpets, settled on what furniture we would get, and adjourned.

Next week I went down to New York and called on the young lady to whom Maurice is engaged. Her home is in New York, or rather it was there; for to my thinking a wife's home is always with her husband; and I never like to hear a wife talking of "going home" as though home could be anywhere else than where her husband and her children are. Maurice and Helen were to be married two weeks from the following Friday, for Maurice proposed to postpone their wedding trip till his next summer's vacation; and Helen, like the dear, sensible girl she is, very readily agreed to that plan. In fact I believe she proposed it. She had some shopping to do before the wedding, and I had some to do on my own account, and we went together. I invented a plan of refurnishing my parlor. I am afraid I told some fibs, or at least came dreadfully near it. I told Helen I wanted her to help me select the carpet; and though she had no time to spare, she was very good-natured, and did spare the time. We ladies had agreed-not without some dissent-to get a Brussels for the parlor, as the cheapest in the end, and I made Helen select her own pattern, without any suspicion of what she was doing, and incidentally got her taste on other carpets, too, so that really she selected them herself without knowing it. Deacon Goodsole recommended me to go for furniture to Mr. Kabbinett, a German friend of his, and Mrs. Goodsole and I found there a very nice parlor set, in green rep, made of imitation rosewood, which he said would wear about as well as the genuine article, and which we both agreed looked nearly as well. We would rather have bought the real rosewood, but that we could not afford. Mr. Kabbinett made us a liberal discount because we were buying for a parsonage. We got an extension table and chairs for the dining-room, (but we had to omit a side-board for the present), and a very pretty oak set for the chamber. We did not buy anything but a carpet for the library, for Mr. Laicus said no one could furnish a student's library for him. He must furnish it for himself.

When we got back to Wheathedge, Tuesday afternoon, we found the parsonage undergoing transformations so great that you would hardly know it. Miss Moore had got Mr. Hardcap, sure enough, to repair it. She had agreed to pay for the material, and he was to furnish the labor. The fence was straightened, and the gate re-hung, and the blinds mended up, and Mr. Hardcap was on the roof patching it where it leaked or threatened to. Deacon Goodsole had a bevy of boys from the Sabbath-school at work in the garden under his direction. If there is anything the Deacon takes a pride in, next to his horse, it is his garden, and he said that the parson should have a chance for the best garden in town. Great piles of weeds stood in the walk. Two boys were spading up; another was planting; a fourth was wheeling away the weeds; and still another was bringing manure from the Deacon's stable. Miss Moore was setting out some rose-bushes before the door; and the Deacon himself, with his coat off, was trimming and tying up a rather dilapidated looking grape-vine over a still more dilapidated grape arbor.

The next morning, about eleven o'clock, little Miss Flidgett came running into our house, without ever knocking, in the greatest possible excitement.

"Mrs. Laicus," said she, "the painters have come."

"The painters!" said I. "What painters?"

"Why didn't you order them?" said she.

"They are painting the parsonage. I supposed of course you ordered them."

It was very evident that she did not suppose anything of the kind, but was dying of curiosity to know who did. I confess I had some curiosity to know myself. So I put on my bonnet and shawl, and ran over with her to find out about it. Sure enough the painters were there, three or four of them, with their ladders up against the side of the house, and the parsonage already beginning to change color under their hands. Some of the ladies were in the kitchen supervising the repairs of the sink, and the putting up of some shelves in the pantry, but they knew nothing about the painters. I asked one of the hands, at work on the front door, who sent him.

"The boss, ma'am," he replied, very promptly.

"And who is the boss?" said I.

"Mr. Glazier, ma'am."

Mr. Glazier is the painter himself, the head-man. So I was no better off than before. I was afraid Mrs. Wheaton had ordered them, and I knew our funds were getting low, for we had overrun our estimate for carpets; and I have the greatest horror of running in debt. So I resolved to go right over to Mrs. Wheaton's and get at the bottom of the mystery. But Mrs. Wheaton knew nothing of the matter. We were both sure Miss Moore would not have ordered them, and I was returning as wise as I started, when, as I passed the parsonage, I saw Mr. Glazier and Mr. Quirk in the yard, talking together. So I turned in to ask Mr. Glazier about it. As I passed up the walk Mr. Quirk called out to me.

"You ladies are in possession, I see," said he. "You mean to make the parson comfortable and contented if you can."

"Yes, Sir," said I, "though we are not responsible for the greatest improvement, the painting. I think Mr. Glazier must be responsible for that himself. I can't find any one that ordered it done."

I thought that would bring the information, and it did.

"Oh! that's Mr. Quirk's orders," said he.

"Yours?" said I turning to the crusty old landlord who wouldn't do anything.

He nodded. I think he enjoyed my perplexity. I spoke on the impulse of the moment. If I had given it a second thought I should not have done it; and yet I am not sorry I did.

"Mr. Quirk," said I, "my husband was right and I was wrong. We ladies thought very hard of you that you would not do anything toward repairing the parsonage. For one I want to apologize."

"Judge not, that ye be not judged," said the old man; and he turned on his heel and went away. He is the queerest man I ever saw.

I wish you could have seen that parsonage last Friday, the day that Mr. Mapleson and his wife were to arrive. The walks were trim. The plot before the piazza had been new sodded. The grapevine was already putting out new buds as if it felt the effect of the Deacon's tender care. There was not a weed to be seen. The beds, with their rich, black loam turned up to the sun, had a beauty of their own, which only one who loves to dig among flowers as much as I do can appreciate. Mr. Glazier had made the dingy old house look like a new one. After all there is nothing I like better for a cottage than pure white with green blinds. Inside we had a lovely carpet on the parlor, and the new set of imitation rosewood. A beautiful bouquet from Mrs. Wheaton's garden stood in the bay window, which looks out upon the river. My girl, lent for the occasion, was in the kitchen; and in the dining-room there was supper spread just for two, with cake, preserves, and pies enough in the closet (every body in the parish had sent in supper for that evening) to keep the parson supplied for a month at least. I was the last to leave the house, and I did not leave it till I heard the whistle of the train. Then I ran over to Miss Moore's little cottage, which is right across the way. Her parlor window was full of ladies peering out, first and foremost of whom was little Miss Flidgett, who thus gratified her wish to see how they would take it. The Deacon, who was fixing something about the stable, was almost caught. But he heard the carriage-wheels just in time to run into the shed, and I could see him there holding the door open a crack and peering out to see what passed. Even dignified Mrs. Wheaton could not resist the temptation to be passing along, accidentally of course, just as the parson drove up. Mr. Wheaton had called for them at the depot. It was arranged (with them, that is) that he was to take them right to our house, and they were to stay there till they could decide whether to board or keep house. He proposed to them, however, according to pre-arrangement, to stop a minute at the parsonage on the way. "Mrs. Mapleson," he said, "can see what it is and how she likes the house, and the location; and besides I have an errand to do at the store."

We saw him get out and hand them out. Just then Mrs. Wheaton passed by, and he introduced her to them. Mrs. Wheaton took a seat in the now vacant carriage to go with her husband to the store; and Mr. and Mrs. Mapleson went up the walk. We saw them go in and shut the door. In a moment they came out again. Maurice looked up and down the street in perplexity; then he stepped back a few paces and looked up at the house. His wife stood meanwhile on the door-step. Suddenly she beckoned to him, and pointed out something on the side of the door just over the bell-handle. They had discovered the little silver plate on which was engraved "Rev. Maurice Mapleson." At that moment the expressman drove up with their trunks. Maurice settled with him, looked up and down the street as if looking for Mr. Wheaton, who did not make his appearance as you may believe; and then parson, wife, and trunks all went into the house together, and we dispersed.

As to the Deacon, he had to climb out of a back window into an ally that runs behind the house in order to get out of his position without being discovered.

And that is the way we gave our donation party in Wheathedge.

CHAPTER XXIV.
Maurice Mapleson.

IT is not six weeks since Maurice Mapleson preached his first sermon here, at Wheathedge, and already events prove the wisdom of our selection. I have been studying somewhat and pondering more the secret of his success, and I have sat down this evening to try and clear up my own shadowy thoughts by reducing them to form. I often take my pen for such a purpose. Is it not Bacon who says the pen makes an accurate thinker?

Maurice Mapleson certainly is not what I should call a great preacher. He is not learned. He is not brilliant. He seldom tells us much about ancient Greece or Rome. He preached a sermon on Woman's function in the church, a few Sundays ago. I could not help contrasting it with Dr. Argure's sermon on the same subject. Maurice could not have made a learned editorial or magazine article out of his sermon. He did not even discuss the true interpretation of Paul's exhortations and prohibitions. He talked very simply and plainly of what the women could do here at Wheathedge.

He thanked them with unmistakeable sincerity for what they had already done, and made it an incentive to them to do more-more for Christ, not for himself.

Jennie says that is the secret of Maurice's success. He is appreciative. He never scolds. He commends his people for what they have done and so incites them to do more. She thinks that praise is a better spur than blame. She always manages her servants on that principle. Perhaps that is the reason why they are not the greatest plague of life to her.

But if Maurice's sermons are not great, neither are they long. He lays it down as a cardinal rule in moral hygiene that a congregation should not go away from the church hungry. Harry no longer begs to stay at home Sunday mornings, and even Mr. Hardcap rarely gets asleep.

If I compare Mr. Mapleson with Mr. Uncannon, I should say unhesitatingly that the latter was the more brilliant preacher of the two. No one ever comes out of church saying "What a powerful discourse! What a brilliant figure! What a pretty illustration! How eloquent!" But I find that we very often spend our dinner hour in discussing not the sermon, but its subject.

There are however two or three peculiarities which I observe about Maurice Mapleson's preaching. Dr. Argure tells me that he never writes a sermon without a reference to its future use. I once asked him whether he ever preached extemporaneously. "No," said he. "I have meant to. But I have so many fine sermons waiting to be preached that I could never bring myself to abandon them for a mere talk."

I do not think Maurice has any fine sermons waiting to be preached. Indeed I know he has not. For one evening when he excused himself from accepting an invitation to tea, because he was behind-hand in his work and had his sermon to prepare, I replied, "You must have a good stock on hand. Give us an old one."

"I haven't a sermon to my name," he replied.

"What do you mean?" said I.

"I mean," said he, "that a sermon is not an essay; that every sermon I ever preached was prepared to meet some special want in my parish, and that when it was preached, there was an end of it. I could no more preach an old sermon than I could fire a charge of gun powder a second time."

"But experiences repeat themselves," said my wife. "What your people at Koniwasset Corners knew of doubt, of trouble, of sorrow, of imperfect Christian experience, we know too. As in water face answereth to face, so the heart of man to man."

"That is true," said Maurice thoughtfully. "But there are no two faces exactly alike. And my sermon is meaningless to me, if not to my people, unless I can see the want and bring out the truth to meet it."

"But the truth is always the same," said Jennie, "and the wants of the human heart are not widely different."

"That is both true and false," said he. "The truth is always the same; but not always the same to me. I fell into conversation with Mr. Gear last night on the subject of the atonement. He thinks it represents God as revengeful and unforgiving. Can I answer him with an old sermon? God's love is immutable. But I hope I understand it better and feel it more than I did three years ago. I cannot bring an old experience to meet a new want. No! a sermon is like a flower, it is of worth only when it is fresh."

His sermons at all events are always fresh. They are his personal counsel to personal friends. I dimly recognize this element of power in them. But this is not all. There is something more, something that I missed in Dr. Argure's learned essays, and in Mr. Uncannon's pulpit pyrotechnics. But it is something very difficult to define.

Did you ever consider the difference between a real flower and a wax imitation? The latter may be quite as beautiful. It may deceive you at first. And yet when you discover the deception you are disappointed. "The lack of fragrance," Jennie suggests. No! the flower may be odorless. It is the lack of life. I do not know what there is in that mystic life that should make such a difference. But I am sure that the charm of the flower is in its life.

The most beautiful statue that Powers ever chiseled does not compare for grace and beauty with the Divine model. The same mystic element of life is wanting.

There is life in Maurice Mapleson's sermons. What do I mean by life? Earnestness? No! Mr. Work was earnest. But this mysterious life was wanting. I can feel it better than I can define it. It is not in the sermon. It is in the man. I get new information from Dr. Argure. I do not get much new information from Maurice Mapleson. I used to get new ideas occasionally from Mr. Work. I rarely get a new idea from Maurice Mapleson. But I get new life, and that is what I most want.

This element of life enters into all his work. It is in the man rather than in his productions.

Our prayer-meetings have improved wonderfully since he came. "How do you prepare for the prayer-meeting?" I asked him the other day.

"By an hour of sleep and an hour of prayer," he replied. "I always try to go into the meeting fresh."

And he succeeds. His coming into the meeting is like the coming of Spring. He brings an atmosphere with him. It is indescribable, but its effect is marvelous. Jennie says she never understood before as she does now what was meant by the declaration in Acts concerning the Apostles, that though they were unlearned men, the people took knowledge of them that they had been with Jesus.

And it is this life which makes him so admirable as a pastor. "Is he social?" a friend asked me the other day. Yes. He is social. But that is not all. Mr. Work was social. But he was always a minister. He went about the streets in a metaphysical white choker and black gown. He was everywhere professional. When he opened the subject of personal religion he did it with an introduction as formal and stately as that with which he habitually began his sermons. He formally inducted you into the witness box and commenced a professional inquisition on the state of your soul. I confess I have no fancy for that sort of Presbyterian confessional. I like the Papal confessional better. It does not invade your house and attack you with its questionings when you are in no mood for them. I told Mr. Work so once, whereat he was greatly shocked and somewhat indignant.

Mr. Uncannon too was very social. But he was never a minister. Outside the pulpit he never introduced the subject of religion. I think it is perfectly safe to say that no one would have taken knowledge of him that he had been with Jesus. As to pastoral calls he expressly disavowed any intention of making any. "I have no time," said he, "for gadding about and spiritual gossiping. It's as much as I can do to get up my two sermons a week."

But Maurice is social in a different way. I asked him once what system he pursued as to pastoral calls.

"A very simple system," said he, "mix much with my people and be much with Christ. If I do both, Mr. Laicus, I shall not fail to bring them together. I don't trouble myself about ways and means."

The week after Mr. Mapleson came to Wheathedge, some ecclesiastical body met at Albany. I had a case before the Court of Appeals, and Maurice and I happened to take the same train. As we waited in the station he addressed himself to a surly looking baggage-master with this question, "What time will the train get to Albany?"

"Can't tell," said the surly baggage-master. "Nothing is certain to railroad men."

"Except one thing," said Mr. Mapleson.

"What's that?" said the surly baggage-master.

"Death," said Mr. Mapleson.

"That's a fact," said the surly baggage-master. "Specially certain to railroad men."

"And there is one other thing certain," added Maurice.

"What's that?" asked the baggage-master, no longer surly.

"That we ought to be ready for it."

The baggage-master nodded thoughtfully. "So we ought," said he; and he added as he turned away, "I hope you're readier than I be."

I note this little incident here because it revealed so much of Maurice Mapleson's character to me. I think it did more to disclose to me the secret of his success than any sermon he has ever preached. Mr. Work when he went away read us the statistics of his ministerial industry. He told us how many sermons he had preached, how many prayer meetings he had attended, how many sick he had visited, and how many religious conversations he had held with the impenitent. I should as soon think of Maurice Mapleson's keeping a record of the number of times he kissed his wife or taught his children-if he had any.

While I have been writing in a vain endeavor to put my vague and shadowy ideas of Maurice Mapleson's magnetic power into words, Jennie has come in and has seated herself beside me.

"Jennie, I cannot get into clear and tangible form my shadowy ideas. What is the secret of ministerial success? What is the common characteristic which gives pulpit power to such widely dissimilar characters as Chalmers, Whitefields, the Westleys, Spurgeon and Robertson in England, and Edwards, Nettleton, Finney, the Beechers, father and son, Murray, John Hall, Dr. Tyng, and a score of others I could mention in this country?"

"Hand me your New Testament, John."

It was lying on the table beside me. She took it from my hand and opened it.

"I don't know as to all the names you have mentioned, John, but I think the secret of true pulpit power, the secret of Paul's wondrous power, the secret of Maurice Mapleson's power--the same in kind though smaller in measure--is this. And she read from Galatians, the second chapter and twentieth verse:

"'I am crucified with Christ, nevertheless I live; yet not I, but Christ liveth in me, and the life which I now live in the flesh, I live by the faith of the Son of God, who loved me, and gave himself for me.'"

CHAPTER XXV.
Our Church-Garden.

ONE needs no other evidence that Maurice Mapleson is working a wonderful transformation in this parish than is afforded by the change which has been made in the external appearance of the church. It is true that Miss Moore always was a worker. But I do not believe that even Miss Moore could have carried out her plan of a church garden under Mr. Work. And Mr. Work was a good minister too.

When I first came to Wheatedge the Calvary Presbyterian church was externally, to the passer-by, distinguished chiefly for the severe simplicity of its architecture, and the plainness, not to say the homeliness, of its surroundings. It is a long, narrow, wooden structure, as destitute of ornament as Squire Line's old fashioned barn. Its only approximation to architectural display is a square tower surmounted by four tooth-picks pointing heavenward, and encasing the bell. A singular, a mysterious bell that was and is. It expresses all the emotions of the neighborhood. It passes through all the moods and inflections of a hundred hearts. To-day it rings out with soft and sacred tones its call to worship. To-morrow from its watch-tower it sees the crackling flame in some neighboring barn or tenement, and utters, with loud and hurried and anxious voice, its alarm. Anon, heavy with grief, it seems to enter, as a sympathising friend, into the very heart experiences of bereaved and weeping mourners. And when the rolling year brings round Independence day, all the fluctuations of feeling which mature and soften others are forgotten, and it trembles with the excitement of the occasion, and laughs, and shouts, and capers merrily in its homely belfry, as though it were a boy again.

Pardon the digression. But I love the dear old bell. And its voice is musical to me, albeit I sometimes fancy, like many another singer's it is growing weak and thin with age.

The surroundings of the church were no better than the external aspect. The fence was broken down. The cows made common pasture in the field-there is an acre of ground with the church, I believe-till the grass was eaten so close to the ground that even they disdained it. A few trees eked out a miserable existence. Most of them, girdled by cattle, were dead. A few still maintained their "struggle for life," but looked as though they pined for the freedom of the woods again. Within, the church justified the promise of its external condition. The board of trustees are poor. Every man had been permitted to upholster his own pew. Some, without owners, were also without upholstering. In the rest, the only merit was variety. The church looked as though it had clothed itself in a Joseph's coat of many colors; or rather, its robe presented the appearance of poor Joe Sweaten's pantaloons, which are so darned and pieced and mended that no man can guess what the original material was, or whether any of it is left. There was but one redeeming feature-the bouquet upon the pulpit. Every Sunday, Sophie Jowett brought that bouquet. As her father had a large conservatory, the bouquet was rarely missing even in winter. As she has admirable taste it was always beautiful even when the flowers were not rare. She had done her work very quietly, had asked no permission, had consulted with no one. One Sabbath the bouquet appeared upon the pulpit. After that it was never missing, except one Sunday when Miss Sophie was sick, and for three weeks in the Fall, when she was away from home.

Such was the condition of the church at Wheathedge when I bought my house.

Last spring Miss Sophie was married. There were more tears and less radiance than usual at that wedding. Mr. Line said that he never could supply the place in the Sunday-school. Mr. Work came up from New York to marry them. His voice was tenderer than usual when he pronounced the marriage ceremony. The first Sabbath after that wedding the pulpit was without flowers. Was there any who did not miss them, and in missing them did not miss her? It took the last ornament from our church, which thenceforth looked desolated enough.

When Maurice Mapleson came the bouquet came back. But it was made mostly of wild flowers. I think his wife began it. Perhaps it was this which suggested to Miss Moore's fertile brain the idea of a church-garden.

At all events one Wednesday after prayer-meeting Miss Moore and Mrs. Biskit came to me. "We want a dollar from you," said Miss Moore.

"What for?" said I. Not that I thought of questioning Miss Moore's demand,-- no one ever does that; but because I naturally liked to know what my money was going to do.

"We are going to start a church-garden," said she. "The trustees have given us the ground, and we want to raise about ten dollars for a beginning."

I gave her the dollar and thought no more about it; indeed, I should have accounted the scheme quite chimerical if there had been any one at the head of it except Miss Moore.

However, the next week, as I was passing the church, I saw Miss Moore and Mrs. Biskit at work in the churchyard. A little plot had been spaded up at one side, one or two walks laid out, and they were busy putting in some flower seed. I thought of offering my services. But as my agricultural education was neglected in my youth, and as my knowledge of gardening is very limited, I passed on.

My chance came pretty soon. When Miss Moore has anything to do for the church every one gets an opportunity to help.

It could not have been more than two or three days later, when, as I passed, I perceived that she had already increased her stock of gardeners. Half a dozen young men were working with a will. She had half of the minister's Bible-class engaged. Two of them had brought a load of gravel from down under the hill as you go to the Mill village. They were shoveling this out at the front gate, while some others were spreading it in a broad walk up to the church-door. A great pile of sods lay right by the side of the growing gravel-heap. Deacon Goodsole, in his shirt sleeves, was raking over the ground preparing it for grass-seed. "Rather late for grass-seed," he had remonstrated, but the inexorable Miss Moore had replied, "Better late than never." Four or five of the boys, who had used the church common as a ball-ground, were enlisted-a capital stroke of policy that. Among them was Bill Styles, who prides himself on throwing a stone higher and with surer aim than any other boy in Wheathedge, and had demonstrated it by stoning all the glass out of the tower windows. A melancholy-looking cow, transfixed with astonishment, had stopped in the middle of the road to look with bewilderment upon their invasion of its ancient territory. I leaned for a moment on the tottering fence and looked, equally bewildered, on the busy scene.

But Miss Moore never suffers any one to look on idly where she is laboring. "Ah! Mr. Laicus," said she, cheerily, "you are just the man we want. That cow will come in through these gaps in the fence and undo our work in an hour after we leave it. I wish you would get hold of somebody and fix it up." With that she was off again, and I was in for an office.

Deacon Goodsole afterwards told me confidentially that he was caught in the same way.

Now, though I am no gardener, I am a bit of a carpenter. So, after taking the dimensions of the fence, mentally, I started off for the material, which Mr. Hard-cap gave, and, with the aid of a volunteer or two, I succeeded in so far filling the breach that the melancholy cow gave up her little game, and walked philosophically away.

To make a long story short, the result of Miss Moore's energetic endeavors was seen the next Sabbath, in part, in an entirely new aspect of affairs, which has been constantly improving since. The board of trustees, moved thereto partly by the energies of Miss Moore, partly by those of their Baptist neighbors who have just got into a new church, have commenced to build a new fence. A graveled walk, free from dust in drought and from mud in rainy weather, leads up to the church-door.

A border of sod on either side melts gradually away into the beginning of a lawn of grass which will be fuller and better next year than this. On a couple of fan shaped lattices, in which I take a little pride as my own handiwork, a honey-suckle on one side of the church-door and a prairie rose on the other are planted. In imagination I already see them reaching out their tendrils in courtship over the door. I should not wonder if next Spring should celebrate their nuptials. Some ivy, planted by Miss Moore, on the eastern side of the church promises in time to embosom it in green. A parterre of flowers in the rear, has already helped to furnish the pulpit every Sunday with a bouquet, and, Miss Moore declares, will, another summer, give the minister a bouquet on his study table all the week, and messengers of beauty to add to the comfort of many a sick-room. And in the Fall Deacon Goodsole and I with half a dozen young men from the pastor's Bible-class are going up into the woods for some maples to set out in the place of the dead sticks which served only as monuments of the departed.

But Miss Moore is in a quandary. She does not know what to do with her ten dollars. All the work was given. Even Pat Maloney, Roman Catholic though he is, would not take anything for spading up the ground for "our church garden."

I am a conservative man. But I do wish Miss Moore could be chairman of our board of trustees for a year or two.

CHAPTER XXVI.
Our Temperance Prayer-Meeting.

IT is late in the fall. The summer birds have fled southward. The summer residents have fled to their city homes. The mountains have blossomed out in all the brilliance of their autumnal colors; but the transitory glory has gone and they are brown and bare. One little flurry of snow has given us warning of what is coming. The furnace has been put in order; the double windows have been put on; a storm-house has enclosed our porch; a great pile of wood lies up against the stable, giving my boy promise of plenty of exercise during the long winter. And still the summer lingers in these bright and glorious autumnal days. And of them the carpenters and the painters are making much in their work on the new library-hall.

Do not let the reader deceive himself by erecting in his imagination an edifice of brick or stone, with all the magnificent architectural display which belongs to the modern style of American cosmopolitan architecture. Library-hall is a plain wooden building, one story high, and containing but three rooms. It is to cost us just $1,000, when it is finished. Let me record here how it came to be begun.

Temperance is not one of the virtues for which Wheathedge is, or ought to be, famous. I know not where you will find cooler springs of more delicious water, than gush from its mountain sides. I know not where you will find grapes for home wine-that modern recipe for drunkenness-more abundant or more admirably adapted to the vintner's purpose. But the springs have few customers, and one man easily makes all the domestic wine which the inhabitants of Wheathedge consume. But at the landing there are at least four grog-shops which give every indication of doing a thriving business, beside Poole's, half-way to the Mill village; to say nothing of the bar the busiest room by all odds, at Guzzem's hotel, busiest, alas! on the Sabbath day.

Maurice Mapleson is not one who considers that his parish and his congregation are coterminus. "I like the Established Church for one thing," he says. "The parish is geographical, not ecclesiastical. All within its bounds are under the parson's care. In our system the minister is only responsible for his own congregation. It is like caring for the wounded who are brought into hospital, and leaving those that are on the field of battle uncared for."

A little incident occurring soon after he came, first opened Maurice's eyes, I think, to the need of temperance reform in the community.

He had occasion, one evening after prayer-meeting, to visit a sick child of his Sabbath-school. The family were poor and his road led him down near the brick-yard toward "Limerick," as this settlement of huts-half house, half pig-stye-is derisively called. The night was dark, and returning, abstracted in thought, he almost fell over what he first took to be a log lying in the street. It was a man, who, on a cursory examination, proved to be suffering under no less a disorder than that of hopeless intoxication. It was a dangerous bed. Maurice made one or two unsuccessful attempts to arouse the fellow, but in vain. Retracing his steps a few rods to the nearest hut, he summoned assistance, and with the aid of Pat sober, got Pat drunk upon his feet. But he was quite too drunk to help himself, and too large and heavy to be left to the sole charge of Pat sober, who happened to recognize a friend, whose home he said was a quarter of a mile down the valley. Maurice, who had preached a few Sundays ago on the parable of the Good Samaritan, could not bring himself to imitate the example of the Priest and Levite; so steadying the tipsy pedestrian on one side, while sober Pat sustained him on the other, they half led, half dragged the still unconscious sleeper to a little round hut, which he called home. The wife was sitting up for her husband and received both him and his custodians with objurgations loud on the first, and thanks equally loud addressed to the others. No sooner was the stupid husband safely deposited on the bed than, begging them to wait a moment, she went to the cupboard and taking down a big, black bottle, half filled a cracked tea-cup with whiskey, which she offered to Maurice as an expression of her gratitude. "I do not know," said Maurice to me, as he told me the story, "that she will ever forgive me for declining, though I couched my declension as courteously as possible."

Coming home and pondering this incident, he made up his mind that something must be done for the temperance cause in Wheathedge; and further pondering led him to the conclusion that he must begin at the church.

So one evening last week he came round to talk with me about it.

"The first thing," said he to me, "is to arouse the Church. I believe in preaching the gospel of temperance to the Jews first, and afterwards to the Gentiles. I will begin in the Synagogue. Afterwards I will go to the streets, and lanes, and highways."

"You will meet with some opposition," said I. "A temperance meeting in the church has never been heard of in Wheathedge. You will be departing from the landmarks."

"Do you think so?" said Maurice.

"I am sure of it," said I.

"Very good," said he, "if I meet with opposition it will prove I am right. It will prove that the Church needs stirring up on the subject. If I am not opposed I shall be inclined to give up the plan. However I will not wait for opportunity I will challenge it."

The next Sunday he gave notice that that evening there would be a Temperance prayer and conference meeting in the church, in lieu of preaching.

"The town," said he, "is cursed with intemperance. There is one miscellaneous dry-goods and grocery store, one drug store, one mill, about half a bookstore, and an ice-cream saloon; and within a radius of half a mile of this church there are ten grog-shops and two distilleries, quite too large a proportion even for those who believe, as I do not, in moderate drinking. I have no remedy to propose. I have no temperance address to deliver. What I do propose is that we gather to-night and make it the subject of earnest prayer to God, and of serious conference among ourselves, that we may know what our duty is in the case, and knowing, may do it bravely and well."

As we came out of church the proposed Temperance prayer-meeting was the theme of general discussion.

Mr. Guzzem was sorry to see that this church was threatened with an irruption of fanaticism. He thought the minister had better stick to his business and leave side-issues alone.

Mr. Wheaton thought the true remedy for intemperance was the cultivation of the grape, and the manufacture of modern wines. He did not believe in meetings.

Mr. Hardcap was as much a foe to intemperance as any one; but he thought the true remedy for intemperance was the preaching of the Gospel. Paul was the model for preachers, and Paul knew nothing but Jesus Christ and Him crucified. Deacon Goodsole inquired who that man was that preached before Felix of righteousness, temperance, and judgment to come. But Mr. Hardcap apparently did not hear the question, at least he did not answer it.

Elder Law thought it might be very well, but that the minister ought not to change the service of the Sabbath without consulting the Session. It was a dangerous precedent.

Deacon Goodsole thought it a move in the right direction, and vowed he would give the afternoon to drumming up recruits. Miss Moore said she would go with him.

Mr. Gear, who has not been inside a prayer-meeting since he has been at Wheathedge, declared when I told him of the meeting, that it was the first sensible thing he had ever known the church to do; and if they were really going to work in that fashion he would like to be counted in. And sure enough he was at the prayer-meeting in the evening, to the great surprise of everybody, and to the consternation of Mr. Hardcap, who found in the fact that an infidel came to the meeting, a confirmation of his opinion that it was a desecration of the Sabbath and the sanctuary.

Mrs. Laynes, whose eldest boy jumped off the dock last Spring in a fit of delirium tremens, came to Maurice with tears in her eyes to thank him for holding a temperance meeting. "I can't do anything but pray," she said; "but oh, Pastor, that I can and will do."

The meeting was certainly a remarkable success, there was just opposition enough to make it so. Those that were determined it should succeed were there ready to speak, to sing, to pray. Those that did not believe in it were there to see it fail. Those that were indifferent were there, curious to see whether it would succeed or fail, and what it would be like. And Deacon Goodsole and Miss Moore were there with their recruits, a curious and motley addition to the congregation. The church was full. Every ear was attention; every heart aroused. And when finally good old Father Hyatt, with his thin white hair and tremulous voice, and eyes suffused with tears, told in tones of unaffected pathos, the sad story of Charl. Pie's death, I do not believe that even Jim Wheaton's eyes were dry. At all events I noticed that when, at the close of the meeting, Maurice put the question whether a second meeting should be held the following month, Jim Wheaton was among those who voted in the affirmative. There were no dissentients.

When I came home from this meeting, I put on paper as well as I could Father Hyatt's pathetic story. It is as follows:

CHAPTER XXVII.
Father Hyatt's Story.

IF you had known Charlie P., and had seen his little struggle, and had felt as I did the anguish caused by his tragic death, you would not talk of moderate drinking as a remedy for intemperance.

I was away from my parish when I first heard of it. I very well remember the start with which I read the first line of the note, "Charlie P-- is dead;" and how after I had finished the account, written in haste and partaking of the confusion of the hour, the letter dropped from my hands, and I sat in the gathering darkness of the summer twilight, rehearsing to myself the story of his life, and the sad, sad story of his tragic death. Years have passed since, but the whole is impressed upon my memory in figures that time cannot fade. If I were an artist, I could paint his portrait, I am sure, as I see him even now. Such a grand, open-hearted, whole-souled fellow as he was.

It was about a year before that I first saw him in my church. His peculiar gait as he walked up the center aisle, first attracted my attention. He carried a stout cane and walked a little lame. His wife was with him. Indeed, except at his office, I rarely saw them apart. She loved him with an almost idolatrous affection; as well she might, for he was the most lovable man I ever knew; and he loved her with a tenderness almost womanly. I think he never for a moment forgot that it was her assiduous nursing which saved his life. His face attracted me from the first, and I rather think I called on the new-comers that very week. At all events we soon became fast friends, and at the very next communion husband and wife united with my church by letter from --, but no matter where; I had best give neither names nor dates. They lived in a quite, simple way, going but little into society, for they were society to each other. They rarely spent an evening out, if I except the weekly prayer-meeting. They came together to that. He very soon went into the Sabbath-school. A Bible-class of young people gathered about him as if by magic. He had just the genial way, the social qualities, and the personal magnetism to draw the young to him. I used to look about sometimes with a kind of envy at the eager attentive faces of his class.

Judge of my surprise when, one day, a warm friend of Charlie's came to me, privately, and said, "Charlie P. is drinking."

"Impossible," said I.

"Alas!" said he, "it is too true. I have talked with him time and again. He promises reform, but keeps no promise. His wife is almost broken-hearted, but carries her burden alone. You have influence with him, more than any one else I think. I want you to see him and talk with him."

I promised, of course. I made the effort, but without success. I called once or twice at his office. He was always immersed in business. I called at his house. But I never could see him alone. I was really and greatly perplexed, when he relieved me of my perplexity. Perhaps he suspected my design. At all events one morning he surprised me by a call at my study. He opened the subject at once himself.

"Pastor," said he, "I have come to talk with you about myself. I am bringing shame on the Church and disgrace on my family. You know all about it. Everybody knows all about it. I wonder that the children do not point at me in the street as I go along. Oh! my poor wife! my poor wife! what shall I do?"

He was intensely excited. I suspected that he had been drinking to nerve himself to what he regarded as a disagreeable but unavoidable duty. I calmed him as well as I could, and he told me his story.

He was formerly a temperate though never a total abstinence man. He was employed on a railroad in some capacity-express messenger I think. The cars ran off the track. That in which he was sitting was thrown down an embankment. He was dreadfully bruised and mangled, and was taken up for dead. It seemed at first as though he had hardly a whole bone in his body; but by one of those marvelous freaks, as we account them, which defeat all physicians' calculations, he survived. Gradually he rallied. For twelve months he lived on stimulants. His wife's assiduous nursing through these twelve months of anxiety prostrated her upon a bed of sickness. From his couch he arose, as he supposed, to go through life on crutches. But returning strength had enabled him to substitute a cane. Her attack of typhoid fever left her an invalid, never to be strong again. Alas! his twelve months' use of stimulants had kindled a fire within him which it seemed impossible to quench.

"I cannot do my work," said he, "without a little, and a little is enough to overset me. I am not a hard drinker, Pastor, indeed I am not. But half a glass of liquor will sometimes almost craze me."

I told him he must give up the little. For him there was but one course of safety, that of total abstinence. He was reluctant to come to it. His father's sideboard was never empty. It was hard to put aside the notions of hospitality which he had learned in his childhood, and adopt the principles of a total abstinence, which he had always been taught to ridicule. However, he resolved bravely, and went away from my study, as I fondly hoped, a saved man.

I had not then learned, as I have since, the meaning of the declaration, "The spirit indeed is willing, but the flesh is weak."

I saw him every few days. He never showed any signs of liquor. I asked him casually, as I had opportunity, how he was getting along. He always answered, "Well."

I sounded others cautiously. No one suspected him of any evil habit. I concluded he had conquered it. Though I did not lose him from my thoughts or prayers, I grew less anxious. He kept his Bible-class, which grew in numbers and in interest. Spring came, and I relaxed a little my labors, as that climate-no matter where it was, to me the climate was bad enough-required it. Despite the caution, the subtle malaria laid hold of me. I fought for three weeks a hard battle with disease. When I arose from my bed the doctor forbade all study and all work for six weeks at least. No minister can rest in his own parish. My people understood that, as parishes do not always. One bright spring day, one of my deacons called, and put a sealed envelope into my hand to be opened when he had left. It contained a check for my traveling expenses, and an official note from the officers of the church bidding me go and spend it. In three days I was on my way to the White Mountains. It was there my wife's hurried note told me the story of Charlie's death. And this was it:

The habit had proved too strong for his weak will. He had resumed drinking. No one knew it but his wife and one confidential friend. He rarely took much; never so much as to be brutal at home, or unfit for business at the office; but enough to prove to him that he was not his own master. The shame of his bondage he felt keenly, powerless as he felt himself to break the chains. The week after I left home his wife left also for a visit to her father's. She took the children, one a young babe three months old, with her. Mr. P. was to follow her in a fortnight. She never saw him again. One night he went to his solitary home. Possibly he had been drinking-no one ever knew-opened his photograph album, covered his own photograph with a piece of an old envelope, that it might no longer look upon the picture of his wife on the opposite page, and wrote her, on a scrap of paper torn from a letter, this line of farewell:

"I have fought the battle as long as I can. It is no use. I will not suffer my wife and children to share with me a drunkard's shame. God-bye. God have mercy on you and me."

The next morning, long after the streets had resumed their accustomed activity, and other houses threw wide open their shutters to admit the fragrance of flowers, and the song of birds, and the glad sunshine, and all the joy of life, that house was shut and still. When the office clerk, missing him, came to seek him, the door was fast. Neighbors were called in. A window was forced open. Lying upon the bed, where he had fallen the night before, lay poor Charlie P. A few drops of blood stained the white coverlet. It oozed from a bullet wound in the back of his head. The hand in death still grasped the pistol that fired the fatal shot.

CHAPTER XXVIII.
Our Village Library.

TO that prayer-meeting and Father Hyatt's story of Charlie P., Wheathedge owes its library.

"Mr. Laicus," said Mr. Gear as we came out of the meeting together, "I hope this temperance movement isn't going to end in a prayer-meeting. The praying is all very well, but I want to see some work go along with it."

"Very well," said I, "what do you propose?"

"I don't know," said he. "But I think we might do something. I believe in the old proverb. The gods help those who help themselves."

That very week Mr. Mapleson called at my house to express the same idea. "What can we do to shut up Poole's?" said he. "It's dreadful. Half our young men spend half their evenings there lounging and drinking away their time." He proposed half a dozen plans and abandoned them as fast as he proposed them. He suggested that we organize a Sons of Temperance, and gave it up because neither of us believed in secret societies; suggested organizing a Band of Hope in the Sabbath-school, but withdrew the suggestion on my remarking that the Sabbath-school would not touch the class that made Poole's bar the busiest place in town; hinted at trying to get John B. Gough, but doubted whether he could be obtained. I told him I would think it over. And the next evening I walked up to Poole's to survey the ground a little. I found, just as you turn the corner from the Main street to go up the hill, what I had never noticed before-a sign, not very legible from old age and dirt, "Free Reading-room." Having some literary predilections, I went in. A bar-room, with three or four loungers before the counter, occupied the foreground. In the rear were two round wooden tables. On one were half a dozen copies of notorious sensation sheets, one or two with infamous illustrations. A young lad of sixteen was gloating over the pages of one of them. The other table was ornamented with a backgammon board and a greasy pack of cards. The atmosphere of the room was composed of the commingled fumes of bad liquor, bad tobacco, kerosene oil and coal gas. It did not take me long to gauge the merits of the free reading-room. But I inwardly thanked the proprietor for the suggestion it afforded me.

"A free reading-room," said I to myself; "that is what we want at Wheathedge."

The same thought had fortunately occurred almost simultaneously to my friend Mr. Korley, though his reason for desiring its establishment were quite different from mine. His family spends every summer at Wheathedge. His wife and daughters found themselves at a loss how to spend their time. They had nothing to do. They pestered Mr. Korley to bring them up the last novels. But his mind was too full of stocks; he always forgot the novels. On Saturday he went over to Newtown, hearing there was a circulating library there. He found the sign, but no books. "I had some books once," the proprietor explained, "but the Wheathedge folks carried them all off and never returned them." Thus it happened that when the week after my visit to the free reading-room, I met Mr. Korley on board the train, he remarked to me, "We ought to have a circulating library at Wheathedge."

"And a reading-room with it," said I.

"Well, yes," said he. "That's a fact. A good reading-room would be a capital thing."

"Think of the scores of young men," said I, "that are going down to ruin there. They have no home, no decent shelter even for a winter's evening, except the grog-shop."

"I don't care so much about the young men," said Mr. Korley, "as I do about the middle-aged ones: My Jennie pesters me almost to death every time I go down, to buy her something to read. Of course I always forget it. Besides, I would like a place where I could see the papers and periodicals myself. I would give fifty dollars to see a good library and reading-room in Wheathedge."

"Very good," said I, "I will put you down for that amount." So I took out my pocket-book and made a memorandum.

"What! are you taking subscriptions?" asked Mr. Korley.

"Have taken one," said I.

That was the beginning. That night I took a blank book and drew up a subscription paper. It was very simple. It read as follows:

"We, the undersigned, for the purpose of establishing a library and reading-room in Wheathedge, subscribe the sums set opposite our names, and agree that when $500 is subscribed the first subscribers shall call a meeting of the others to form an organization."

I put Mr. Korley's name down for $50, which started it well. Mr. Jowett could do no less than Mr. Korley, and Mr. Wheaton no less than Mr. Jowett; and so, the subscription once started, grew very rapidly, like a boy's snowball, to adequate proportions. The second Tuesday in July I was enabled to give notice to all the subscribers to meet at my house. My parlors were well filled. I had taken pains to get some lady subscribers, and they were there as well as the gentlemen. I read to the company the law of the State providing for the organization of a library association. Resolutions were drawn up and adopted. Stock was fixed at $5, that everybody might be a stockholder. The annual dues were made $2, imposed alike on stockholders and on outsiders. A Board of trustees was elected. And so our little boat was fairly launched.

We began in a very humble way. The school trustees loaned us during the summer vacation a couple of recitation-rooms which we converted into a library and conversation-room. The former we furnished in the first instance with the popular magazines and two or three of the daily newspapers. We forthwith began also to accumulate something of a library. Mr. Wheaton presented us with a full assortment of Patent Office reports, which will be very valuable for reference if any body should ever want to refer to them. We also have two shelves full chiefly of old school-books, which a committee on donations succeeded in raising in the neighborhood.

But apart from these treasures of knowledge our collection is eminently readable. Maurice Mapleson is on the library committee, and Maurice Mapleson is fortunately a very sensible man. "The first thing," he says, "is to get books that people will read. Valuable books that they won't read may as well stay on the publishers' shelves as on ours." So as yet we buy only current literature. We rarely purchase any book in more than two volumes. We have a good liberal assortment of modern novels-but they are selected with some care. We sprinkle in a good proportion of popular history and popular science. The consequence is our library is used. The books really circulate. Our conversation-room has proved quite as popular as the library. It is furnished with chess and checkers. What is more important it is furnished with young ladies. For the Wheathedge library knows neither male nor female. And the young men find our checkers more attractive than Tom Poole's cards. They are ready to exchange the stale tobacco smoke and bad whiskey of his bar-room for the fair, fresh faces that make our reading-room so attractive. The boys, too, as a class are very willing to give up the shameless pictorial literature of his free reading-room for Harper's and the Illustrated Christian Weekly. In a word the Wheathedge library became so universally popular that when the opening of the school threatened to crowd us out of our quarters, there was no difficulty in raising the money to build a small house, large enough for our present and prospective needs. The only objection was Mr. Hardcap. For Mr. Hardcap does not approve of novels.

This objection came out when I first asked him for a subscription, payable in work on the new building.

"Do you have novels in your library?" said he.

"Of course," said I.

"Then," said he, "don't come to me for any help. I won't do anything to encourage the reading of novels."

"You do not approve of novels, then, I judge, Mr. Hardcap?" said I.

"Approve of novels!" said he, energetically. "If I had my way, the pestiferous things should never come near my house. I totally condemn them. I don't see how any consistent Christian can suffer them. They're a pack of lies, anyhow."

"Do you not think," said I, "that we ought to discriminate; that there are different sorts of novels, and that we ought not to condemn the good with the bad?"

"I don't believe in no kind of fiction, nohow," said Mr. Hardcap, emphatically. "What we want is facts, Mr. Laicus-hard facts. That's what I was brought up on when I was a boy, and that's what I mean to bring my boys up on."

I thought of Mr. Gradgrind, but said nothing.

"Yes," said Mr. Hardcap, half soliloquizing, "there is Charles Dickens. He was nothing in the world but a novel writer, and they buried him in Westminster Cathedral, as though he were a saint; and preached sermons about him, and glorified him in our religious papers. Sallie is crazy to get a copy of his works, and even wife wants to read some of them. But they'll have to go out of my house to do it, I tell ye. Why, they couldn't make more to do if it was Bunyan or Milton."

"Bunyan?" said I. "Do you mean the author of Pilgrim's Progress?"

"Yes," said he: "that is a book. Why, it's worth a hundred of your modern novels."

"How is that?" said I. "Pilgrim's Progress, if I mistake not, is fiction."

"Oh! well," said .Mr. Hardcap, "that's a very different thing. It isn't a novel. It's a allegory. That's altogether different."

"What is the difference?" said I.

"Oh! well," said he, "that's altogether different. I suppose it is fictitious; but then it's altogether different. It's a allegory."

"Now I don't approve," continued Mr. Hardcap, without explaining himself any further, "of our modern Sunday-school libraries. I have complained a good deal, but it's no use. Tom brings home a story book every Sunday. I can't very well say he shan't take any books out of the library, and I don't want to take him out of Sunday-school. But I don't like these Sunday-school stories. They are nothing but little novels anyhow. And they're all lies. I don't believe in telling stories to teach children. If I had my way, there wouldn't be but one book in the library. That would be the Bible."

"You could hardly leave in all the Bible," said I. "You would have to cross out the parable of the prodigal son."

"The parable of the prodigal son!" exclaimed Mr. Hardcap, in astonishment.

"Yes," said I: "that is, if you did not allow any fiction in your Sunday reading."

"Oh!" said he, "that's very different. That's not fiction; that's a parable. That's entirely different. Besides," continued he, "I don't know what right you have to assume that it is a story at all. I have no doubt that it is true. Christ says distinctly that a man had two sons, and one came and asked him for his portion. He tells it all for a fact, and I think it very dishonoring to him to assume that it is not. I have no doubt that he knew just such a case."

"And the same thing is true of the parable of the lost sheep, and the lost piece of money, and the sower, and the merchantman, and the pearl, and the unfaithful steward?" I asked.

"Yes," said he, "I have no doubt of it."

"Well," said I, "that is at least a new view of Scripture teaching."

"I have no doubt it is the correct one," said he. "I don't believe there is any fiction in the Bible at all."

"Well," said I, "when you get home you read Jotham's story of the trees, in the Book of Judges; I think it's about the ninth chapter."

"I will," said he; "but if it's in the Bible I have no doubt it is true, no doubt whatever."

But in spite of Mr. Hardcap, the Wheathedge library flourished; and next week our new quarters are to be dedicated to the cause of literature and temperance by a public meeting. And I am assured by those that know, that Tom Poole's business was never so poor as it has been since we started our opposition to his free reading-room.

Miss Moore asked Maurice Mapleson last week to suggest a subject for an illuminated motto to hang on the wall of the reading-room over the librarian's desk.

"Overcome evil with good," said he.

CHAPTER XXIX.
Maurice Mapleson Tries an Experiment.

FIVE or six weeks ago Maurice came to me in some excitement. "Mr. Laicus," said he, "is it true that ten of you gentlemen have to contribute thirty dollars a piece this year to make up my salary?"

"No," said I.

"Why, John," said Jennie.

"We didn't have to do it," I continued. But in point of fact we do it."

"I don't like that," said he soberly. "If the church can't pay me fifteen hundred dollars a year I do not want to receive it. I thought the church was strong and well able to do all it professed to do."

"My dear Mr. Mapleson," said I, "you attend to the spiritual interests of the church and leave its finances to us. If we cannot pay you all we have promised, we will come and beg off. Till then you just take it for granted that it's all right."

Maurice shook his head.

"Why, my dear friend," said I, "how much do you suppose I pay for pew rent?"

"I haven't the least idea," said he.

"Fifty dollars," said I. "That provides myself and wife and Harry with a pew in church twice on the Sabbath if we want it. It pays for Harry's Sabbath-school instruction and for your service as a pastor to me and to mine. But we will make no account of that. Fifty dollars a Sabbath is a dollar a week, fifty cents a service, twenty cents a head. Harry half price, and the Sabbath-school, and the prayer-meetings, and the pastoral work thrown in. It is cheaper than any lecturer would give it to us, and a great deal better quality too. My pew rent isn't what I pay for the support of the Gospel. It is what I pay for my own spiritual bread and butter. It won't hurt me, nor Deacon Goodsole, nor Mr. Wheaton, nor Mr. Gowett, nor any one else on that list to contribute thirty dollars more for the cause of Christ and the good of the community."

Maurice shook his head thoughtfully, but said nothing more about it then, and the matter dropped.

The last week in December we have our annual meeting. It is generally rather a stupid affair. The nine or ten gentlemen who constitute the board of trustees meet in the capacity of an ecclesiastical society. In the capacity of a board of trustees they report to themselves in the capacity of a society. In the capacity of a society they accept the report which they have presented in the capacity of a board of trustees, and pass unanimously a resolution of thanks to the board, i. e. themselves, for the efficient and energetic manner in which they have discharged their duties. They then ballot in a solemn manner for themselves for the ensuing year and elect the ticket without opposition. And the annual meeting is over.

But this year our annual meeting was a very different affair. The Sabbath preceding, the parson preached a sermon on the text: "The poor have the Gospel preached to them." In this sermon he advocated a free-pew system. His arguments were not very fresh or new (there is not much that is new to be said on the subject) till he came to the close. Then he startled us all by making the following proposition:

"The chief objection," said he, "to the free-pew system is the question, 'Where shall the money come from?' From God, I answer. I believe if we feed his poor, he will feed us. I, for one, am willing to trust Him, at least for one year."

It slipped out very naturally, and there was a little laugh in the congregation at the preacher's expense. But he was very much in earnest.

"I propose to the society to throw open the doors of this church, and declare all the pews free. Provide envelopes and papers, and scatter them through the pews. Let each man write thereon what he is willing to pay for the support of the Gospel, and whether he will pay it weekly, monthly, quarterly, semi-quarterly or annually. Give these sealed envelopes to me. No one shall know what they contain but myself and the treasurer. I will pay out of the proceeds all the current expenses of the church, except the interest. Whatever remains, I will take as my salary. The interest, the trustees will provide out of the plate collections and with the aid of the ladies. This is my proposition. Consider it seriously, earnestly, prayerfully, and come together next Wednesday night to act intelligently upon it."

I hardly think the minister's eloquence would have sufficed to carry this plan, but the treasurer's balance-sheet helped his case amazingly.

I supposed there would be a small deficit, but thought I knew it could not be very great. But I had not reckoned on the genius for incapacity which characterises church boards. To have the unusual deficit, which was involved by the increase of the parson's salary, provided for by a special subscription was more than they could bear. They had regarded it as their duty, made plain by the example of their predecessors in office for many years, to bring the church in debt, and nobly had they fulfilled their duty. On the strength of that extraordinary subscription they had rushed into extraordinary expenditures with a looseness that was marvellous to behold.

Here is the annual exhibit as it appears in the treasurer's report:

BALANCE SHEET. Cr. Pew-rents $1,250.00 Sunday Collections 325.25 Received by a Ladies' Fair 113.34 Special Subscription 300.00

$1,988.59

Dr. Minister's Salary $1,500.00 Organist (a new expenditure advocated by Mr. Wheaton because of the Special Subscription), Six months' salary 100.00 Church Repairs, (a new fence and new blinds, &c., advocated by Mr. Wheaton because of the Special Subscription) 134.75 Reed Organ for the Sabbath-School (advocated by Mr. Wheaton because of the Special Subscription) 150.00 Interest on Mortgage 315.00 Sexton 200.00 Fire, lights and incidentals 225.00 Commission for collecting pew-rents 55.75

   $2,680.50

   1,988.59 Deficit $691.91

Of course, the minister's salary was behind; and, of course, the minister was behind to the grocer, and the baker, and the butcher, and the dry-goods dealer; and, of course, everybody felt blue. There was a good deal of informal discussion before the parson's proposition was taken up. Mr. Hardcap wanted to decrease the minister's salary. Mr. Wheaton wanted to raise the pew rents. Mr. Leacock thought Mr. Wheaton could afford to give up his mortgage on the church. Mr. Line proposed to take up a subscription, pay the balance off on the spot, and begin the new year afresh. Mr. Gazbag thought it ought to be left to the ladies to clear off the debt with a concert or something of that sort. Mr. Cerulian thought (though he said it very quietly) that if we had a minister who could draw better, we shouldn't have any difficulty.

The parson kept his own counsel till these various plans had been, one after another, proposed and abandoned. Then he again proposed his own.

"I do not want," he said, "any more salary than this church and congregation can well afford to give. I am willing if it is poor to share its poverty. I believe if it is prosperous it will be willing to share with me its prosperity. I have studied this matter a good deal; I believe the pew rent system to be thoroughly bad. It excludes the poor. What is more to the purpose it excludes those whom we most need to reach. The men who most need the Gospel will not pay for it. The law of supply and demand does not apply. No man pays a pew rent who does not already at least respect religion, if he does not personally practise it. The influence within the church of selling the Gospel in open market is as deadly as its influence without. It creates a caste system. Practically our pews are classified. We have a parquette, a dress circle, a family circle, and an amphitheatre. The rich and poor do not meet together. We are not one in Christ Jesus. Moreover I believe it to be as bad financially as it is morally. When an American makes a bargain he wants to make a good one. What he buys he wants to get as cheap as his neighbor. If you rent your pews, every renter expects to get his seat at the lowest rates. But Americans are liberal in giving. If they contributed to the support of the Gospel, if what they gave the church was a free gift, I believe they would give with a free hand. At all events I would like to try the experiment. It can be no worse than it has been this year. The trustees can have no difficulty in raising interest money from the plate collections and a special subscription. There can be no injustice in requiring them to secure a special fund for any special expenditures. And all the other expenditures I will provide for myself out of the free gifts of the congregation. I am willing to run all the risks. It may do good. It can do the church no harm."

A long discussion followed this proposal.

Mr. Wheaton was at first utterly opposed to the plan. He thought it was tempting Providence to make no more adequate provision for our debts. Six of us quietly agreed to assume the mortgage debt, that is to say to insure him that the plate collections and the ladies together would pay the interest promptly. That changed his view. He said that if the minister had a mind to risk his salary on such a crazy scheme, very well. And at the last he voted for it.

Mr. Hardcap thought it was a first-rate plan. It was noticed afterward that he moved from a plain seat in the gallery to a cushioned and carpeted seat in the center aisle. Whether he paid any more contribution than he had before paid of pew rent, nobody but the parson knows. But nobody suspects him of doing so.

Mrs. Potiphar thought it was horrid. What was to prevent any common, low-born fellow, any carpenter's son, right from his shop, coming and sitting right alongside her Lillian? She couldn't sanction such communist notions in the church.

Deacon Goodsole warmly favored the minister's idea-was its most earnest advocate, and was the man who first started the plan for buying Mr. Wheaton's acquiescence.

Mr. Line hadn't a great deal of faith in it. This was not the way the church used to raise money when he was a boy. Still, he wanted to support the minister, and he wanted to have the poor reached, and he hadn't anything to say against it.

Squire Rawlins said, "Go ahead. The minister takes all the risk, don't you see? He's a big fool in my opinion. But there's no law agin a man makin' a fool of himself, ef he wants ter."

Miss Moore organized that very night a double force to carry the plan into effect. One was a ladies' society to pay the interest; the other was a band of workers, young men and young women, to go out on Sunday afternoons and invite the people who now do not go anywhere to church, to come to ours.

On the final vote the plan was carried without a dissenting voice. I beg Mrs. Potiphar's pardon. Her voice was heard in very decided dissent as the meeting broke up. But as the ladies do not vote in the Calvary Presbyterian Church, her protest did not prevent the vote from being unanimous.

Maurice Mapleson is sanguine of results, I am not. I am afraid he will come out bankrupt himself at the end of the year. I wanted to raise a special subscription quietly to ensure his salary. But he would not hear of it. He replied to my suggestion, "I said I would trust the Lord, and I will. If you want to add to your envelope contribution, very well. But I do not want any more than that will give me."

But one thing I notice and record here. Our congregation have increased from ten to twenty per cent. Miss Moore's invitations have met with far greater success than I anticipated. I never could get any of the boys from the Mill village to come to church at all regularly under the old system. When this change was made I gave notice of it, and now over half my Bible-class are in the congregation. But I can get no intimation from Maurice how the plan is prospering financially. All he will say is, "We shall all know at the close of the year."

CHAPTER XXX.
Mr. Hardcap's Family Prayers.

"JENNIE," said I, the other evening, "I should like to go and make a call at Mr. Hardcap's."

Our new pastor had preached a sermon on that unapplied passage of Scripture, Luke xiv: 12-14. It had made a great stir in our little village. Mr. Wheaton thought it was a grand sermon, but impracticable. Mrs. Potiphar resented it as personal. Deacon Goodsole thought it was good sound doctrine. I thought I would give the sermon a trial; meanwhile I reserved my judgment.

It is not a bad method, by the way, of judging a sermon to try it and see how it works in actual experiment.

Jennie assented with alacrity to my proposition; her toilet did not take long, and to Mr. Hardcap's we went.

It was very evident that they did not go into society or expect callers. In answer to our knock we heard the patter of a child's feet on the hall floor and Susie opened the door. As good fortune would have it, the sitting-room door at the other end of the hall stood invitingly open, and so, without waiting for ceremony, I pushed right forward to the common room, which a great blazing wood fire illuminated so thoroughly that the candles were hardly necessary. Mrs. Hardcap started in dismay to gather up her basket of stockings, but on my positive assurance that we should leave forthwith if she stopped her work she sat down to it again. Luckily the night was cold and there was no fire in the stove of the cheerless and inhospitable parlor. So they were fain to let us share with them the cheery blaze of the cozy sitting-room. We did not start out till after seven, and we had not been in the room more than ten minutes before the old-fashioned clock in the corner rang out the departure of the hour and ushered in eight o'clock--whereat James laid aside his book, and at a signal from his father brought him the family Bible.

"We always have family prayers at eight o'clock," said Mr. Hardcap, "before the children go to bed; and I never let anything interfere with it."

This in the tone of a defiant martyr; as one under the impression that we were living in the middle ages and that I was an Inquisitor ready to march the united family to the stake on the satisfactory evidence that the reading of the Bible was maintained in it.

I begged him to proceed, and he did so, the defiant spirit a little mollified.

He opened at a mark somewhere in Numbers. It was a chapter devoted to the names of the tribes and their families. Poor Mr. Hardcap! If he was defiant at the first threatening of martyrdom, he endured the infliction of the torture with a resolute bravery worthy of a covenanter. The extent to which he became entangled in those names, the new baptism they received at his hands, the singular contortions of which he proved himself capable in reproducing them, the extraordinary and entirely novel methods of pronunciation which he evolved for that occasion, and the heroic bravery with which he struggled through, awoke my keenest sympathies. Words which he fought and vanquished in the first paragraph rose in rebellion in a second to be fought and vanquished yet again. The chapter at length drew to an end. I saw to my infinite relief that he was at last emerging from this interminable feast of names. What was my horror to see him turn the page and enter with fresh zeal upon the conquest of a second chapter.

Little Charlie (five years old) was sound asleep in his mother's arms. Her eyes were fixed on vacancy and her mind interiorly calculating something. I wondered not that James snored audibly on the sofa. Susie never took her eyes off her father, but sat as one that watches to see how a task is done. My wife listened for a little while with averted face, then wandered off, as she afterwards told me, to a mental calculation of her resources and expenses for the next month. And still Mr. Hardcap rolled out those census tables of Judea's ancient history. It was not till he had finished three chapters that at length he closed the book and invited me to lead in prayer.

Half an hour later, after Jamie had been roused up from his corner of the sofa and sent off to bed, and Charlie had been undressed and put to bed without being more than half aroused, Mrs. Hardcap asked my advice as to this method of reading the Bible.

"Mr. Hardcap," said she, "read a statement the other day to the effect that by reading three chapters every day and five on Sunday he could finish the Bible in a year. And he is going through it in regular course. But I sometimes doubt whether that is the best way. I am sure our children do not take the interest in it which they ought to; and I am afraid those chapters of hard names do not always profit me."

The martyr in Mr. Hardcap re-asserted itself.

"All Scripture," said he solemnly, "is given by inspiration of God and is profitable for doctrine, for reproof, for correction and for instruction in righteousness. We cannot afford to pass by any part of the word of God."

"What do you think about it, Mr. Laicus?" said Mrs. Hardcap.

"Think!" said I; "I should be afraid to say what I think lest your husband should account me a hopeless and irreclaimable unbeliever."

"Speak out," said Mr. Hardcap; "as one who at the stake should say, 'pile the fuel on the flame, and try my constancy to its utmost.' "Where the spirit of the Lord is, there is freedom."

"Well," said I, "if I were to speak out, I should say that this way of reading the Bible reminds me of the countryman who went to a city hotel and undertook to eat right down the bill of fare, supposing he ought not to call for fish till he had eaten every kind of soup. It is as if one being sick, should go to the apothecary's shop, and beginning on one side, go right down the store taking in due order every pill, po-tion, and powder, till he was cured-or killed."

Mr. Hardcap shook his head resolutely. "Is it not true," said he, "that all Scripture is profitable?"

"Yes," said I, "but not that it is all equally profitable for all occasions. All the food on the table is profitable, but not to be eaten at one meal. All the medicine in the apothecary's shop is profitable, but not for the same disease."

"There is another thing," said Mrs. Hardcap, "that I cannot help being doubtful about. James is learning the New Testament through as a punishment."

"As a punishment!" I exclaimed.

"Yes," said she. "That is, Mr. Hardcap has given him the New Testament, and for his little offences about the house he allots him so many verses to learn; sometimes only ten or twelve, sometimes a whole chapter. I am afraid it will give the poor boy a distaste for the word of God."

"There is no danger," said Mr. Hardcap, oracularly. "The word of God is sharper than a two edged sword, and is quick even to the dividing asunder of the joints and the marrow. It is the book to awaken conviction of sin, the proper book for the sinner. There is no book so fitting to bring him to a sense of his sinfulness and awaken in him a better mind."

"And how," said I, "do you find it practically works? Does he seem to love his Bible?"

"Says he hates it awfully," said his mother.

"Such," said Mr. Hardcap, "is the dreadful depravity of the human heart. It is deceitful above all things, and desperately wicked."

It was quite idle to argue with Mr. Hardcap. We left him unconvinced, and I doubt not he is still reading his three chapters a day and five on Sunday. But I pity poor James from the bottom of my heart; and as my wife and I walked home I could not but help contrasting in my own mind Mr. Hardcap's way of reading the Bible and that which Deacon Goodsole pursues in his family.

CHAPTER XXXI.
In Darkness.

LAST Tuesday night Jennie met me at the station. It is unusual for her to do so. The surprise was a delightful one to me. But as I sat down beside her in the basket wagon she did not greet me as joyously as usual. Her mien was so sober that I asked her at once the question:

"Jennie, what is the matter? You look sick."

"I am sick, John," said she; "sick at heart. Willie Gear is dead."

"Willie Gear dead!" I exclaimed.

"Yes," said Jennie. "He was skating on the pond. I suppose this warm weather has weakened the ice. It gave way. Three of the boys went in together. The other two got out. But Willie was carried under the ice."

Jennie was driving. Instead of turning up the hill from the depot she kept down the river road. "I thought you would want to go down there at once," said she. "And so I left baby with Nell and came down for you."

We rode along in silence. Willie Gear was his father's pride and pet. He was a noble boy. He inherited his mother's tenderness and patience, and with them his father's acute and questioning intellect. He was a curious combination of a natural skeptic and a natural believer. He had welcomed the first step toward converting our Bible-class into a mission Sabbath-school, and had done more than any one else to fill it up with boys from the Mill village. He was a great favorite with them all and their natural leader in village sports and games. There was no such skater or swimmer for his age as Willie Gear, and he was the champion ball-player of the village. But I remember him best as a Sabbath-school scholar. I can see even now his earnest upturned face and his large blue eyes, looking strait into his mother's answering gaze, and drinking in every word she uttered to that mission-class which he had gathered and which she every Sabbath taught. He was not very fortunate in his teacher in our own church Sabbath-school. For he took nothing on trust and his teacher doubted nothing. I can easily imagine how his soul filled with indignation at the thought of Abraham's offering up his only son as a burnt sacrifice, and how with eager questioning he plied his father, unsatisfied himself with the assurances of one who had never experienced a like perplexity, and therefore did not know how to cure it.

And Willie was really gone. Would it soften the father's heart and teach him the truth of Pascal's proverb that "The heart has reasons of its own that the reason knows not of;" or would it blot out the last remnant of faith, and leave Mr. Gear without a God as he had been without a Bible and without a Saviour?

I was still pondering these problems, wildly thinking, not aimlessly, yet to no purpose, when we reached the familiar cottage. Is it indeed true that nature has no sympathy? There seemed to me to be on all around a hush that spoke of death. There needed no sorrowful symbol of crape upon the door; and there was none. I almost think I should have known that death was in the house had no one told me.

As I was fastening my horse Mr. Hardcap came up. We entered the gate together.

"This is a hard experience for Mr. Gear," said I to Mr. Hardcap.

"The judgments of the Lord are true and righteous altogether," replied Mr. Hardcap, severely.

I could feel Jennie tremble on my arm, but I made no response to Mr. Hardcap.

Mr. Gear opened the door for us himself before we had time to knock. He was perfectly calm and self-possessed. Jennie said afterward she should not have guessed, to have seen him elsewhere, that he had even heard of Willie's death. But I noticed that he uttered no greeting. He motioned us into the sitting-room without a word.

Here, on a sofa, lay, like a white statue, the form of the dear boy. By the side of the sofa sat the mother, her eyes red and swollen with much weeping. But the fierceness of sorrow had passed; and now she was almost as quiet as the boy whose sleep she seemed to watch; she was quite as pale.

She rose to meet us as we entered, and offered me her hand. Jennie put her arm around the poor mother's waist and kissed her tenderly. But still nothing was said.

Mr. Hardcap was the first to break the silence. "This is a solemn judgment," said he.

Mr. Gear made no reply.

"I hope, my friend," continued Mr. Hardcap, "that you will heed the lesson God is a teachin' of you, and see how fearful a thing it is to have an unbeliev'n heart. God will not suffer us to rest in our sin of unbelief. If we lay up our treasures on earth where moth and rust doth corrupt, we must expect they will take to themselves wings and fly away."

Mr. Hardcap's horrible mutilation of Scripture had always impressed me in a singular manner. But I think its ludicrous side never so affected me before. What is it in me that makes me always appreciate most keenly the ludicrous in seasons of the greatest solemnity and distress? The absurdity of his misapplication of the sacred text mingled horribly with a sense of the insupportable anguish I knew he was causing. And yet I knew not how to interfere.

"I hope he was prepared," said Mr. Hardcap.

"I hope so," said Mr. Gear quietly.

"He was such a noble fellow," said Jennie to the weeping mother. She said it softly, but Mr. Hardcap's ears caught the expression.

"Nobility, ma'am," said he, "isn't a savin' grace. It's a nateral virtoo. The question is, did he have the savin' grace of faith and repentance?"

"I believe," said Mrs. Gear, earnestly, "that Willie was a Christian, if ever there was one, Mr. Hardcap."

"He hadn't made no profession of religion you know, ma'am," said Mr. Hardcap. "And the heart is deceitful above all things and desperately wicked."

Mr. Hardcap is very fond of quoting that text. I wonder if he ever applies it to himself.

"It seems kind o' strange now that he should be taken away so sudden like," continued Mr. Hardcap, "without any warnin'. And you know what the Scripture tells us. 'The wages of sin is death.'"

Mr. Gear could keep silence no longer. "I wish then," said he hoarsely, "God would pay me my wages, and let me go."

"Oh! Thomas," said his wife appealingly. Then she went up to Mr. Hardcap, and laid her hand gently on his arm. "Mr. Hardcap," said she, "it was very good of you to call on us in our sorrow. And I am sure that you want to comfort us, and do us good. But I don't believe my husband will get any good just now from what you have to say. We are stunned by the blow that came so suddenly, and must have a little time to recover from it. Would you feel offended if I asked you to go away and call again some other time?"

"The word must be spoken in season and out of season," said Mr. Hardcap doggedly. Nevertheless he turned to leave. He offered his hand to Mr. Gear, who was leaning with his head upon his hand against the mantel-piece, and possibly did not notice the proffered salutation. At all events he never moved. Mr. Hardcap looked at him a moment, opened his mouth as if to speak, but apparently reconsidered his purpose, for he closed it again without speaking, and so left the room. Mrs. Gear went with him to the door, where I heard her ask him to pray for her and for her husband, and where I heard him answer something about a sin unto death that could not be prayed for. Jennie followed Mrs. Gear softly out; and so Mr. Gear and I were left alone.

Alone with the dead.

"That's your Christian consolation," said Mr. Gear bitterly.

"Is that just to your wife?" I answered him quietly.

"No! It is not just to my wife," he replied. "I would give all I possess to have her faith. She is almost heart-broken,--and yet-yet-I who ought to sustain her would be crazed with grief if I had not her to lean upon. And she-she leans on I know not what. Oh! if I did but know."

"She leans on Him who not in vain Experienced every human pain," I answered softly.

"He was such a noble boy," continued Mr. Gear speaking half to himself, and half to me. "He was so pure, so truthful, so chivalrous, so considerate of his mother's happiness and of mine. And he was beginning to teach me, teach me that I did not know all. I was afraid of my own philosophy for him. I wanted him to have his mother's faith, though I never told him so. I never perplexed him with my own doubtings. I solved what I could of his, I was coming to believe little by little that there was a clearer, better light than that I walked in. I was hoping that he might find it and walk in it. I even dreamed, sometimes, to myself, that he would yet learn how to show it to me. And now he is gone, and the glimmer of light is gone, and the last hope for me is gone with him."

"He is gone," I said softly, "to walk in that clearer, better light, and beckons you to follow."

Mr. Gear made no answer, hardly seemed to note the interruption.

"And this is the bitterness of the blow to me," he continued, still speaking half to me, half to himself. "I thought I believed in immortality. I thought I believed in God. These two beliefs at least were left me. And now nothing is left. My wife says 'he is not dead but sleepeth.' But I cannot see it. To me he is gone, for ever gone. If on the other side of that veil which hides him from me, that mystic something which we call his spirit still lingers, I do not see it. I had a dream of that better land once and called it faith. But this cruel blow has wakened me, and the dream has passed in the very hour when I need it most. And nothing is left me; not even that poor vision."

"Not even God?" said I softly.

"Not even God," he answered with terrible deliberation. "For a bad God is worse than no God at all. And how can I believe that God is good? He looks down on our happy home. He looks on our dear boy, its life and joy. He knows how our life is wrapped up in him. He sees how little by little Willie is leading me up into a higher, happier, holier life. And then He strikes him down, and leaves my wife heart-broken, and me in darkness, bereft by one blow of my child and of my faith."

Then he pointed to the dead boy who lay on the lounge before us. "How can I reconcile this with the love of God?" he cried. "How can you, Mr. Laicus?"

All bitterness was gone now. He looked me earnestly in the eye, and asked eagerly, as one who longed for a solution, and yet was in despair of finding it.

"I cannot," I answered, "and dare not try. If I had only life's book to read, Mr. Gear, I should not believe in a God of love. I should turn Persian, and believe in two gods, one of love and good-will, one of hate and malice."

He looked at me in questioning surprise.

"Love, Mr. Gear, is its own demonstration. I know that God loves me."

"How?" said he.

"How?" said I. "Do you remember when we first met, Mr. Gear, that you told me your God was everywhere, in every brook, and mountain, and flower, and leaf, and storm, and ray of sunshine."

He nodded his head reflectively, as one recalling a half forgotten conversation.

"My God is in the hearts of those that seek Him," said I. "And in my heart I carry an assurance of His love that life cannot disturb. I know His love as the babe knows its mother's love, lying upon her breast. It knows her love though it neither understands her nature nor her ways."

He shook his head sadly.

"Mr. Laicus," said he, "I believe you, but I do not comprehend you. I believe that you have a faith that is worth the having. I would give all I possess or ever possessed to share it with you in this hour. I do not know-I sometimes think it is only a pleasant dream. Would God I could sleep and dream such dreams."

"It is no dream, Mr. Gear, but truth and soberness," said I. "A dream does not last through eighteen centuries, and raise half a world from barbarism to civilization. A dream does not carry mothers through such sorrows as this with outlooking anticipations so clear as those which give Mrs. Gear her radiant hope. No! Mr. Gear. It is you who have been dreaming, and life's sorrow has awakened you."

"Mr. Laicus," he cried almost passionately, "I said I believed in nothing. But it is not true. I have no creed. I do not even believe in God or immortality any more. I have no God. I am without hope. But I believe in my wife. I believe in you. I believe that you and she have something-I know not what-that supports you in temptation and sustains you in sorrow. Tell me what it is. Tell me how I may get it. I will cast my pride away. I would believe. Help my unbelief."

"Mr. Gear," said I, laying my hand upon his arm, "here in the presence of this dear boy, be the solemn witness of your petition and your vow, will you kneel with me to ask of God what you have asked of me, but what He alone can give you, and record before Him the promise you have made to me, but which He alone can receive at your hands?"

He made no answer-hesitated a moment-then knelt, with the dear boy's hand fast clasped in his, while kneeling at his side I echoed the prayer he had already uttered: "I believe; help Thou mine unbelief."

And as we rose I saw the tears streaming down his softened face, the first tears he had shed since I had entered his house. I knew that Willie had taught him more in his death than by his life, and felt that now, to my own heart though not to his, I could answer the question he had asked me, "How can you reconcile this with the love of God?"

CHAPTER XXXII.
God said, "Let there be Light."

FROM Mr. Gear's Jennie and I drove directly to Maurice Mapleson's. Fortunately we found him at home. Briefly I told him of my visit.

"What can we do," I said at the close, "to save this man from the despair of utter skepticism?"

"He is in good hands," said Mr. Mapleson, with calm assurance.

"No! Mr. Mapleson," said I, "I can do nothing more with him. So long as I had only the intellect to deal with, I thought I knew what to say and when to keep silence. But I dare neither speak nor keep silence now."

"I did not mean your hands," said Mr. Mapleson.

"What then?" said I.

"He is in God's hands," replied the pastor. "God has taken him out of your hands into His own. Leave him there."

"Is there then nothing more to be done?" I said.

"Yes," said he, "but chiefly prayer."

Then after a moment's pause he added: "I believe, Mr. Laicus, in the oft quoted and generally perverted promise: If two of you shall agree on earth as touching anything that they shall ask, it shall be done for them of my Father which is in heaven. I believe it was intended for just such exigencies as this. It is not a general charter, but a special promise. Now is the time to plead it. Who beside yourself in our church is Mr. Gear's most intimate acquaintance and warmest friend?"

I thought a moment before I answered. Then I replied, "To be honest, Mr. Mapleson, I do not believe there is one in the church who understands him. But Deacon Goodsole has had more to do with him than any other, and perhaps understands him better."

"Very well," said Mr. Mapleson. "Will you meet Deacon Goodsole at my house to-morrow evening, half an hour before the prayer-meeting, to unite in special prayer for Mr. Gear? I will see the Deacon. I am sure he will come."

"I am sure he will," I added warmly; "as sure as that I will be there myself."

With that I bade Mr. Mapleson good-night and hurried away. For tea had long been waiting, the children's bed hour was near, and Jennie was growing impatient to be at home.

Wednesday evening Mr. Mapleson, the Deacon and I went into our church prayer-meeting from half an hour spent in Mr. Mapleson's study in prayer for Mr. Gear. Mr. Mapleson had seen Mr. Gear that morning. But the stricken father was very silent; he offered no communication; and Mr. Mapleson had pressed for none. I confess I had hoped much from Mr. Mapleson's interview, and I went into the prayer-meeting burdened and sorrowful.

I think I have already remarked that Mr. Mapleson's conduct of a prayer-meeting is exceedingly simple. He seldom says much. He sets us all an example of brevity. A few words of Scripture, a few earnest words of his own or a simple prayer, usually constitute his sole contribution to the meeting, which is more truly a meeting for prayer than any other prayer-meeting I ever attended.

That evening he seemed loath to open the meeting. We were little late in beginning. When we did begin we were late in getting into the heart of it. He called on one after another to lead in prayer. I did not know but that he was going to omit the reading of Scripture and his own remarks altogether. Our prayer-meeting commences at half-past seven. The pastor never allows it to overrun an hour. And it was after eight when he arose to read. He read from the twelfth chapter of Acts, the account of Peter's deliverance from prison. He read it from beginning to end without a comment, and then he spoke substantially as follows. His words were very simple. But that meeting has left an impression upon me that time will never obliterate. I believe I could repeat his words to my dying day.

"A great deal is said and written," said he, "about the apostolic faith. But the apostles were men of like passions as we ourselves. They fought the same doubts. They prayed in the same hesitating, uncertain, unbelieving way. Peter was in prison. His friends could do nothing to effect his deliverance-nothing but pray. So they assembled for that purpose. They had the promise of the Lord, 'If two of you shall agree on earth as touching anything that they shall ask, it shall be done for them of my Father which is in Heaven.' But they did not believe it. They took some comfort in praying-as we do. But they did not expect any answer to their prayers. The thought that God might really afford deliverance never seems to have occurred to them. And when Peter, delivered by the angel of the Lord, came knocking at the gate of the house, and the startled disciples wondered what this midnight summons might mean, and the servant returned to report that Peter stood without, they laughed at her. You are mad, said they. And when he persisted in his knocking, and she in her assertion, they added with trembling and under-breath to one another, in mortal fear, "It is his ghost." Anything was more credible to their minds than that God should have answered their united prayers.

"The promise of God is to the prayer of faith. But God is constantly better than his promise. He does not limit Himself by our expectations. He does exceedingly abundantly more than we can ask or even think. We are not therefore to be driven from our knees by our want of faith. I hear men talk as though prayer were of no avail unless we believe beforehand with assurance that we were going to receive all for which we asked. It is not true. We are not heard for our much asking, nor for much our believing, but for God's great mercy's sake.

"When the mission was first started at the Mill village, if I have understood aright, it was started on the application of the children themselves. They gathered around the school-house when the Bible-class assembled. They had no expectation of instruction. When the first person came to the door to invite them in, probably half of them scampered away in fright. Did they expect all that has come? Or would any Christian worker have said, 'They shall not have a Sabbath-school till they ask it, and believe that it will be provided for them?' And our Father does not wait for the prayer of faith. Like the father in the parable he comes while we are yet afar off. If we have faith enough to look wistfully and yearningly for a blessing, He has superabundant love to grant it."

And then he read, and we sang that most beautiful hymn:

"Oh! see how Jesus trusts himself
Unto our childish love!
As though by His free ways with us
Our earnestness to prove.
His sacred name a common word

On earth He loves to hear;
There is no majesty in Him
Which love may not come near.
The light of love is round His feet,
His paths are never dim;
And He comes nigh to us when we
Dare not come nigh to Him.
Let us be simple with Him, then,
Not backward, stiff, nor cold,
As though our Bethlehem could be
What Sinai was of old."

Mr. Mapleson is very fond of music. Singing is a feature of all our prayer-meetings. I have heard him say that he thought more people had been sung into the kingdom of heaven than were ever preached into it. Usually his rich voice carries the bass almost alone. But during the singing of this hymn he sat silent, leaning his head upon his hand. This silence was so unusual that it almost oppressed the meeting. When the hymn closed there was a solemn hush, a strange expectancy; it seemed as though no one dared to break the sacred silence.

Our lecture-room occupies half the basement of the church. I sat in a front seat, close by the little desk-a low platform furnished only with a light stand on which rests the minister hymn-book and a small Bible. The room was full, but it had filled up after I came in.

The prolonged silence grew painful. Then I heard a rustle as of one rising to his feet. Then a voice; I startled, half turned round, restrained myself, thank God, and only cast on Jennie, at my side, a look of wonder and of thanksgiving. The voice was that of Mr. Gear.

"Fellow-townsmen," said he,--he spoke hesitatingly at first as one unused to the place and the assemblage,--"I have come here to make a request. You are surprised to see me here. You will be more surprised to hear my request. I want to ask you to pray for me."

He had recovered from his hesitancy now. But he spoke with an unnatural rapidity as though he were afraid of breaking down altogether if he stopped a moment to reflect upon himself and his position.

"You know me only as an infidel. I am an infidel. At least I was. Yes! I suppose I still am. My mother died when I was but a babe. My father brought me up. He was orthodox of the orthodox. But oh! he was a hard man. And he had a hard creed. I used to think the creed made the man. Lately I have thought perhaps the man made the creed. At all events both were hard. And I repudiated both. At fourteen I abhorred my father's creed. At eighteen I had left my father's roof. I have never returned except on occasional visits."

He had gained more self-possession now, and spoke more slowly and distinctly. The room was as still as that room of death in which the evening before I had prayed with him, kneeling by the corpse of his little boy.

"What I have been at Wheathedge you know. I cannot come here to-night on a false pretence. I cannot call myself a desperate sinner. I have wronged no man. I have lived honestly and uprightly before you all. I owe no man anything. I have depended on my daily labor for my daily bread. Out of it I have provided as I had opportunity for the poor around me. No one ever went hungry from my door away. My creed has been a short and simple one, 'Do unto others as you would have others do unto you.' I have tried to live according to my creed.

"But I begin to think that my creed is not all the truth. Mr. Laicus first led me to think so. No! my boy first led me to think so. I was satisfied with my creed for myself. But I was not satisfied with it for my boy.

"Then I met Mr. Laicus. We commenced to study the Bible together. If he had attempted to prove my opinions wrong I would have defended them. But he did not. We studied the undoubted truth. The doubtful points he left alone. I learned there was more in the Bible, more in human life and the human heart than I had thought. I grew little by little sure that I had not all the truth. But I was unwilling to confess it. I was-yes, I was too proud.

"Yesterday"--his voice trembled and he spoke with difficulty for a moment, but quickly recovered himself--"yesterday we lost the light and life out of our house. No! I am wrong. My light was extinguished, and my life was quenched in death. But my wife's was not. The dear boy was as dear to her as he was to me. But she lives and hopes; I am in darkness and almost in despair. My father's hard creed drove me into infidelity. My wife's, my friend's tenderer and happier faith calls me back again. But

I do not know the way.

"Last night, kneeling by the side of my dear boy, I vowed that I would cast away my pride and seek that light in which my wife and my friends are walking. An hour ago the thought occurred to me-where seek it better than where they are gathered who are walking in this light? It seemed to me I could not come. But I had made the vow. I would not go back from it. I have cast away my pride. Oh! friends, help me to find that light in which you walk.

"Do not misunderstand me. I will not have your prayers on false pretences. I am, if not still an infidel, at least an unbeliever. I have no creed. I only believe that there is light somewhere, for others live in it. And I long to come into that light myself. Help me to find the way. And yet-I hardly know why I came here to-night. It was not for counsel. I do not want words now. The kindliest only pain me. Discussion and debate would arouse all the old devil of contradiction in me. Leave me alone. No! Do not leave me alone. Give me your prayers. Give me your Christian sympathies. But for the rest, for a little while, I want to be alone."

He sat down. There was a moment of perfect stillness. Then the pastor arose.

"Christ's sympathies are broader and His love is larger than we think," said he. "We hedge him round with our poor creeds, and shut Him up in our little churches, and think He works only in our appointed ways. He breaks over the barriers we put about him, and carries on His work of love in hearts that we think are beyond all reach of Him or us. We cannot tell our brother how to find the light. The light will find him. 'Jesus Christ is the light which lighteth every man that cometh into the world.' And when the heart casts its pride away the light enters. For thus saith the High and Lofty One that inhabiteth eternity, whose name is Holy; I dwell in the high and holy place; with him also that is of a contrite and humble spirit, to revive the heart of the contrite ones. Into His hands let us commit our brother's spirit."

And he poured forth his soul in a prayer which carried heavenward many an unbreathed cry for help, and received in the beating of many hearts a warmer, truer response than any spoken words could have given to it.

After service I walked along with Maurice Mapleson.

"I was never more astonished in my life," said I, "than when I heard Mr. Gear's voice in the prayer-meeting to-night."

"I was not astonished," said Mr. Mapleson. "I went to that prayer-meeting sure that God had in store for us a better answer to our prayers than we had thought. I do not believe in presentiments; but I had a strange presentiment that Mr. Gear would come to our meeting to-night, that God would rebuke our little faith by His unexpected answer. I even waited for Mr. Gear's coming. I saw him enter. I took that chapter of Acts-which God seemed to give me at the moment-partly that I might lead him on to fulfil the purpose which I fully believed had brought him there. While you were singing, I was praying. And when the hymn and the prayer were ended together, I knew God would not let him go away unblest."

"I shall never again doubt," said I, "the truth of God's promise-'that if two of us shall agree on earth as touching anything they shall ask, it shall be done for them.'"

"Shall you not?" said he, with a smile. "I wish I could be as sure for myself."

CHAPTER XXXIII.
A Retrospect.

I am sitting in my library. The fire burns cheerily in the grate. A dear voice is singing sweetly by my side. For baby is restless to-night and Jennie has brought him down to rock him to sleep here and keep me company.

The years pass in review before me. Thank God for the dear wife who three years ago persuaded me that I was a Christian more than a Congregationalist. The years have not been unfruitful. The work has been, oh! so little, and the harvest so great!

I believe the whole church is satisfied with the result of our peculiar method of candidating. I am sure there is no one who would willingly exchange Mr. Mapleson for Mr. Uncannon. There have been rumors once or twice that there was danger Maurice Mapleson would leave. He has twice had invitations to preach in city churches whose pulpits were vacant. But he has declined. "I hope," he says, "to live and die here. It is as God wills. But I have no ambition for a larger field of usefulness. It is all I can do to cultivate this field."

My prophesy has proved true respecting Mr. Work. He has broken down, given up preaching, nominally because of a throat trouble; really, I believe, because of spirit trouble, and has opened a young ladies' school in one of the suburbs of the city. Mr. Uncannon has left North Bizzy after a year's pastorate, for one of the great cities of the West, where he is about equally famous for his fast horses, his good cigars, and his extraordinary pulpit pyrotechnics.

Maurice Mapleson's experiment has proved a complete success. Our church at last is out of its financial difficulties. We held our annual meeting last week. And here is the financial exhibit as it appeared in the treasurer's report:

Cr. Monthly Subscriptions $1,675.00 Sunday Collections 395.85 Ladies' Entertainments (a special fair having been organized by Miss Moore to secure the interest money.) 251.06

$2,321.91

2,276.90 Balance in Treasury $45.01

Dr. Minister's Salary $1,500.00 Organist, (the office was discontinued, congregational singing established, and Deacon Goodsole's eldest daughter volunteered to play.) Nothing Church Repairs-Sundries 55.50 Interest on Mortgage 315.00 Sexton (Salary reduced by himself as a contribution to the support of the church.) 175.00 Fire, lights and incidentals 231.40

$2,276.90

The church has never before had a balance in its treasury, and it was bewildered with astonishment at the result. The money was really due to Maurice, who was to pay, the reader will recollect, the incidental expenses out of the monthly subscriptions and take the remainder as his salary. But Maurice positively refused to take it. He, however, has long wanted the old pulpit cut down and a low platform substituted. The money was voted for that purpose, and the alterations are now going on.

Though the pews are free, the pew system is not wholly abandoned. Each attendant selects a seat for himself or a pew for his family. This is regarded his as much as if he paid pew rent for it. But instead of a fixed rent he pays what he will. No one has paid less than the old rates and some have nearly doubled them. But the improvement in finances is not the only nor even the best result of Maurice Mapleson's experiment. The congregation has increased quite as much as the income. Not less than a score of families are regular attendants on our church who never went to church before. With one or two exceptions every pew is taken. We are beginning to talk quietly about an enlargement.

I think this change had something to do with the revival last Spring. Maurice thinks so at all events. And any attempt to go back to the old system would meet with as much opposition from Deacon Goodsole as from Jim Wheaton. The only member of the congregation who regrets the change is Mrs. Potiphar. She turns up her nose --metaphorically I mean--the natural nose is turned up all the time at that revival. "It did not reach any of our set," she says. "Why, bless you, I don't believe it added fifty dollars to the church income."

One would think to hear her talk that Mrs. Potiphar supported the church. If she does, her right hand does not know what her left hand is doing.

The immediate precursor of that revival was the prayer-meeting which Mr. Gear attended, and in which he asked the prayers of the church. When in June he stood up before the congregation to profess his faith in Christ as a Savior from sin, and in the Holy Spirit as a Divine Comforter in trial and in sorrow, he did not stand alone. Twenty-eight stood with him. Among them were nine of the boys from our Mill village Bible-class. Of that brightest of Sabbath days I cannot trust myself to speak. The tears come to my eyes, and my hand trembles as I write. I must pass on to other thoughts.

I have already explained how the Bible-class gathered to itself a second class of which Mrs. Gear took charge. Both classes have grown steadily, and latterly, rapidly, and are now beyond all that the most sanguine of us ever anticipated. There is a flourishing Sabbath-school at the Mill village. Mr. Gear superintends it. Nearly half of my old scholars are teachers now. But others have come to take their places. My own class is larger than ever. Once a month Mr. Mapleson preaches in the school-house, and in the summer his congregation overflows upon the green sward without. Once or twice he has been forced into the grove adjoining. It is evident that the old school-house will not serve us much longer. Mr. Gear is already revolving plans for the erection of a chapel. It seems to me rather chimerical. No! On second thoughts nothing seems to me chimerical any more. And as Mr. Gear and Miss Moore are both engaged in this enterprize, I am confident it will succeed.

There is not in our church a more active, earnest, devoted Christian worker than Mr. Gear. He is one of the board of trustees, and about the only man on it who is not afraid of Jim Wheaton. He rarely misses a prayer-meeting, and though he does not speak very often he never speaks unless he has something to say. And that is more than can be said of some of those who "occupy the time" in our prayer-meetings. I understand that Mr. Hardcap was not altogether satisfied with Mr. Gear's "evidences" when he appeared before the session. But if daily life affords the true "evidences" of Christian character, there are very few of us that might not be glad to exchange with Mr. Gear. I doubt whether Dr. Argure would think he was sound in the faith. And if the "faith" is synonymous with the Westminster Assembly's Confession of it, I do not believe he is. Deacon Goodsole has confidentially hinted to me his fear that Mr. Gear has some doubts concerning the doctrine of election; and that he is not quite clear even on the doctrine of eternal punishment. It is not impossible. But I do not believe there is a member of our church whose faith in a present, prayer-hearing God is stronger. His first step toward securing a chapel for the Sabbath-school has been taken already. It was a meeting of the Sabbath-school teachers at his own house to pray for a chapel. And he builds on that prayer-meeting a strong assurance that he will get it. I do not think he is quite sound in the catechism. I wish I were as sound in the faith.

I have often wished to know how he solved his old doubts. If I could find his specific for skepticism, I thought to myself, it would be of inestimable value to others. So with some hesitation, lest I should awaken the old unbelief, I asked him the question the other day.

"How did you finally settle your old difficulties concerning Christian truth?" said I.

"I never have," said he quietly. "They disappeared of themselves, as the snow disappears from Snow-cap when May comes."

The fire burns low upon the hearth. The risen moon casts her soft light through the Eastern window and bathes the room with her radiance. The mountains, mist clad, stand as shadows of their daily self, more beautiful in their repose than in the full glory of the busy day. The baby sleeps quietly, nestled close to his mother's breast, too big I tell her for her arms; but she protests I'm wrong. And still I sit, silent, and the past defiles before me.

At length Jennie breaks the silence. "What are you pondering so deeply, John?"

"I was thinking, Jennie, how much I owe the little woman who persuaded me to this dear home, who convinced me that I was, or at least ought to be, a Christian more than a Congregationalist, and who taught me that I could work for Christ without infringing on my daily duties, and so brought to me all the flood tide of happiness that makes my life one long song of joy."

THE END.

The Codes Of Hammurabi And Moses
W. W. Davies

QTY

The discovery of the Hammurabi Code is one of the greatest achievements of archaeology, and is of paramount interest, not only to the student of the Bible, but also to all those interested in ancient history...

Religion   **ISBN:** *1-59462-338-4*   **Pages:132**
MSRP *$12.95*

The Theory of Moral Sentiments
Adam Smith

QTY

This work from 1749. contains original theories of conscience amd moral judgment and it is the foundation for systemof morals.

Philosophy **ISBN:** *1-59462-777-0*   **Pages:536**
MSRP *$19.95*

Jessica's First Prayer
Hesba Stretton

QTY

In a screened and secluded corner of one of the many railway-bridges which span the streets of London there could be seen a few years ago, from five o'clock every morning until half past eight, a tidily set-out coffee-stall, consisting of a trestle and board, upon which stood two large tin cans, with a small fire of charcoal burning under each so as to keep the coffee boiling during the early hours of the morning when the work-people were thronging into the city on their way to their daily toil...

Pages:84

Childrens   **ISBN:** *1-59462-373-2*   **MSRP *$9.95***

My Life and Work
Henry Ford

QTY

Henry Ford revolutionized the world with his implementation of mass production for the Model T automobile. Gain valuable business insight into his life and work with his own auto-biography... "We have only started on our development of our country we have not as yet, with all our talk of wonderful progress, done more than scratch the surface. The progress has been wonderful enough but..."

Pages:300

Biographies/   **ISBN:** *1-59462-198-5*   **MSRP *$21.95***

The Art of Cross-Examination
Francis Wellman

QTY

I presume it is the experience of every author, after his first book is published upon an important subject, to be almost overwhelmed with a wealth of ideas and illustrations which could readily have been included in his book, and which to his own mind, at least, seem to make a second edition inevitable. Such certainly was the case with me; and when the first edition had reached its sixth impression in five months, I rejoiced to learn that it seemed to my publishers that the book had met with a sufficiently favorable reception to justify a second and considerably enlarged edition. ...

Pages:412

Reference   ISBN: *1-59462-647-2*   *MSRP $19.95*

On the Duty of Civil Disobedience
Henry David Thoreau

QTY

Thoreau wrote his famous essay, On the Duty of Civil Disobedience, as a protest against an unjust but popular war and the immoral but popular institution of slave-owning. He did more than write—he declined to pay his taxes, and was hauled off to gaol in consequence. Who can say how much this refusal of his hastened the end of the war and of slavery?

Law   ISBN: *1-59462-747-9*   Pages:48
MSRP $7.45

Dream Psychology Psychoanalysis for Beginners
Sigmund Freud

QTY

Sigmund Freud, born Sigismund Schlomo Freud (May 6, 1856 - September 23, 1939), was a Jewish-Austrian neurologist and psychiatrist who co-founded the psychoanalytic school of psychology. Freud is best known for his theories of the unconscious mind, especially involving the mechanism of repression; his redefinition of sexual desire as mobile and directed towards a wide variety of objects; and his therapeutic techniques, especially his understanding of transference in the therapeutic relationship and the presumed value of dreams as sources of insight into unconscious desires.

Pages:196

Psychology   ISBN: *1-59462-905-6*   *MSRP $15.45*

The Miracle of Right Thought
Orison Swett Marden

QTY

Believe with all of your heart that you will do what you were made to do. When the mind has once formed the habit of holding cheerful, happy, prosperous pictures, it will not be easy to form the opposite habit. It does not matter how improbable or how far away this realization may see, or how dark the prospects may be, if we visualize them as best we can, as vividly as possible, hold tenaciously to them and vigorously struggle to attain them, they will gradually become actualized, realized in the life. But a desire, a longing without endeavor, a yearning abandoned or held indifferently will vanish without realization.

Pages:360

Self Help   ISBN: *1-59462-644-8*   *MSRP $25.45*

The Rosicrucian Cosmo-Conception Mystic Christianity by *Max Heindel* ISBN: *1-59462-188-8* **$38.95**
The Rosicrucian Cosmo-conception is not dogmatic, neither does it appeal to any other authority than the reason of the student. It is: not controversial, but is: sent forth in the, hope that it may help to clear... New Age/Religion Pages 646

Abandonment To Divine Providence by *Jean-Pierre de Caussade* ISBN: *1-59462-228-0* **$25.95**
"The Rev. Jean Pierre de Caussade was one of the most remarkable spiritual writers of the Society of Jesus in France in the 18th Century. His death took place at Toulouse in 1751. His works have gone through many editions and have been republished... Inspirational/Religion Pages 400

Mental Chemistry by *Charles Haanel* ISBN: *1-59462-192-6* **$23.95**
Mental Chemistry allows the change of material conditions by combining and appropriately utilizing the power of the mind. Much like applied chemistry creates something new and unique out of careful combinations of chemicals the mastery of mental chemistry... New Age Pages 354

The Letters of Robert Browning and Elizabeth Barret Barrett 1845-1846 vol II ISBN: *1-59462-193-4* **$35.95**
by *Robert Browning* and *Elizabeth Barrett* Biographies Pages 596

Gleanings In Genesis (volume I) by *Arthur W. Pink* ISBN: *1-59462-130-6* **$27.45**
Appropriately has Genesis been termed "the seed plot of the Bible" for in it we have, in germ form, almost all of the great doctrines which are afterwards fully developed in the books of Scripture which follow... Religion/Inspirational Pages 420

The Master Key by *L. W. de Laurence* ISBN: *1-59462-001-6* **$30.95**
In no branch of human knowledge has there been a more lively increase of the spirit of research during the past few years than in the study of Psychology, Concentration and Mental Discipline. The requests for authentic lessons in Thought Control, Mental Discipline and... New Age/Business Pages 422

The Lesser Key Of Solomon Goetia by *L. W. de Laurence* ISBN: *1-59462-092-X* **$9.95**
This translation of the first book of the "Lernegton" which is now for the first time made accessible to students of Talismanic Magic was done, after careful collation and edition, from numerous Ancient Manuscripts in Hebrew, Latin, and French... New Age/Occult Pages 92

Rubaiyat Of Omar Khayyam by *Edward Fitzgerald* ISBN:*1-59462-332-5* **$13.95**
Edward Fitzgerald, whom the world has already learned, in spite of his own efforts to remain within the shadow of anonymity, to look upon as one of the rarest poets of the century, was born at Bredfield, in Suffolk, on the 31st of March, 1809. He was the third son of John Purcell... Music Pages 172

Ancient Law by *Henry Maine* ISBN: *1-59462-128-4* **$29.95**
The chief object of the following pages is to indicate some of the earliest ideas of mankind, as they are reflected in Ancient Law, and to point out the relation of those ideas to modern thought. Religiom/History Pages 452

Far-Away Stories by *William J. Locke* ISBN: *1-59462-129-2* **$19.45**
"Good wine needs no bush, but a collection of mixed vintages does. And this book is just such a collection. Some of the stories I do not want to remain buried for ever in the museum files of dead magazine-numbers an author's not unpardonable vanity..." Fiction Pages 272

Life of David Crockett by *David Crockett* ISBN: *1-59462-250-7* **$27.45**
"Colonel David Crockett was one of the most remarkable men of the times in which he lived. Born in humble life, but gifted with a strong will, an indomitable courage, and unremitting perseverance... Biographies/New Age Pages 424

Lip-Reading by *Edward Nitchie* ISBN: *1-59462-206-X* **$25.95**
Edward B. Nitchie, founder of the New York School for the Hard of Hearing, now the Nitchie School of Lip-Reading, Inc, wrote "LIP-READING Principles and Practice". The development and perfecting of this meritorious work on lip-reading was an undertaking... How-to Pages 400

A Handbook of Suggestive Therapeutics, Applied Hypnotism, Psychic Science ISBN: *1-59462-214-0* **$24.95**
by *Henry Munro* Health/New Age/Health/Self-help Pages 376

A Doll's House: and Two Other Plays by *Henrik Ibsen* ISBN: *1-59462-112-8* **$19.95**
Henrik Ibsen created this classic when in revolutionary 1848 Rome. Introducing some striking concepts in playwriting for the realist genre, this play has been studied the world over. Fiction/Classics/Plays 308

The Light of Asia by *sir Edwin Arnold* ISBN: *1-59462-204-3* **$13.95**
In this poetic masterpiece, Edwin Arnold describes the life and teachings of Buddha. The man who was to become known as Buddha to the world was born as Prince Gautama of India but he rejected the worldly riches and abandoned the reigns of power when... Religion/History/Biographies Pages 170

The Complete Works of Guy de Maupassant by *Guy de Maupassant* ISBN: *1-59462-157-8* **$16.95**
"For days and days, nights and nights, I had dreamed of that first kiss which was to consecrate our engagement, and I knew not on what spot I should put my lips..." Fiction/Classics Pages 240

The Art of Cross-Examination by *Francis L. Wellman* ISBN: *1-59462-309-0* **$26.95**
Written by a renowned trial lawyer, Wellman imparts his experience and uses case studies to explain how to use psychology to extract desired information through questioning. How-to/Science/Reference Pages 408

Answered or Unanswered? by *Louisa Vaughan* ISBN: *1-59462-248-5* **$10.95**
Miracles of Faith in China Religion Pages 112

The Edinburgh Lectures on Mental Science (1909) by *Thomas* ISBN: *1-59462-008-3* **$11.95**
This book contains the substance of a course of lectures recently given by the writer in the Queen Street Hail, Edinburgh. Its purpose is to indicate the Natural Principles governing the relation between Mental Action and Material Conditions... New Age/Psychology Pages 148

Ayesha by *H. Rider Haggard* ISBN: *1-59462-301-5* **$24.95**
Verily and indeed it is the unexpected that happens! Probably if there was one person upon the earth from whom the Editor of this, and of a certain previous history, did not expect to hear again... Classics Pages 380

Ayala's Angel by *Anthony Trollope* ISBN: *1-59462-352-X* **$29.95**
The two girls were both pretty, but Lucy who was twenty-one who supposed to be simple and comparatively unattractive, whereas Ayala was credited, as her Bombwhat romantic name might show, with poetic charm and a taste for romance. Ayala when her father died was nineteen... Fiction Pages 484

The American Commonwealth by *James Bryce* ISBN: *1-59462-286-8* **$34.45**
An interpretation of American democratic political theory. It examines political mechanics and society from the perspective of Scotsman James Bryce Politics Pages 572

Stories of the Pilgrims by *Margaret P. Pumphrey* ISBN: *1-59462-116-0* **$17.95**
This book explores pilgrims religious oppression in England as well as their escape to Holland and eventual crossing to America on the Mayflower, and their early days in New England... History Pages 268

QTY

The Fasting Cure *by Sinclair Upton* ISBN: *1-59462-222-1* **$13.95**
In the Cosmopolitan Magazine for May, 1910, and in the Contemporary Review (London) for April, 1910, I published an article dealing with my experiences in fasting. I have written a great many magazine articles, but never one which attracted so much attention... New Age/Self Help/Health Pages 164

Hebrew Astrology *by Sepharial* ISBN: *1-59462-308-2* **$13.45**
In these days of advanced thinking it is a matter of common observation that we have left many of the old landmarks behind and that we are now pressing forward to greater heights and to a wider horizon than that which represented the mind-content of our progenitors... Astrology Pages 144

Thought Vibration or The Law of Attraction in the Thought World ISBN: *1-59462-127-6* **$12.95**

by William Walker Atkinson Psychology/Religion Pages 144

Optimism *by Helen Keller* ISBN: *1-59462-108-X* **$15.95**
Helen Keller was blind, deaf, and mute since 19 months old, yet famously learned how to overcome these handicaps, and spread her lectures promoting optimism. An inspiring read for everyone... Biographies/Inspirational Pages 84

Sara Crewe *by Frances Burnett* ISBN: *1-59462-360-0* **$9.45**
In the first place, Miss Minchin lived in London. Her home was a large, dull, tall one, in a large, dull square, where all the houses were alike, and all the sparrows were alike, and where all the door-knockers made the same heavy sound... Childrens/Classic Pages 88

The Autobiography of Benjamin Franklin *by Benjamin Franklin* ISBN: *1-59462-135-7* **$24.95**
The Autobiography of Benjamin Franklin has probably been more extensively read than any other American historical work, and no other book of its kind has had such ups and downs of fortune. Franklin lived for many years in England, where he was agent... Biographies/History Pages 332

Name	
Email	
Telephone	
Address	
City, State ZIP	

☐ **Credit Card**   ☐ **Check / Money Order**

Credit Card Number	
Expiration Date	
Signature	

Please Mail to: Book Jungle
                        PO Box 2226
                        Champaign, IL 61825
or Fax to: 630-214-0564

ORDERING INFORMATION

web*: www.bookjungle.com*
email*: sales@bookjungle.com*
fax*: 630-214-0564*
mail*: Book Jungle PO Box 2226 Champaign, IL 61825*
or PayPal *to sales@bookjungle.com*

Please contact us for bulk discounts

DIRECT-ORDER TERMS

**20% Discount if You Order
Two or More Books**
Free Domestic Shipping!
Accepted: Master Card, Visa,
Discover, American Express